W9-BYH-870

Dangerous Girls
The Taste of Night

Dangerous Girls

The Taste of Night

A NOVEL BY

R.L. STINE

TITLE V
FY 05

■ HarperCollins*Publishers*
A Parachute Press Book

Library of Congress Cataloging-in-Publication Data
Stine, R.L.
    Dangerous girls : the taste of night / by R.L. Stine.— 1st ed.
    p. cm.
    Sequel to: dangerous girls.
    Summary: Livvy Weller wants her twin sister, Destiny, to join her on the darker side as a vampire, but Destiny is determined to restore Livvy to her human condition and bring her back home to their family.
    ISBN 0-06-059616-3 — ISBN 0-06-059617-1 (lib. bdg.)
    [1. Vampires—Fiction. 2. Sisters—Fiction. 3. Twins—Fiction.] I. Title.
PZ7.S86037Dap 2004   2004002151
[Fic]—dc22

Typography by Sasha Illingworth
1 2 3 4 5 6 7 8 9 10
❖
First Edition

For Susan Lurie, still dangerous after all these years.

CONTENTS

part one: july

CHAPTER ONE: My Sister is a Vampire   3

CHAPTER TWO: "Can You Kill Your Own Daughter?"   8

CHAPTER THREE: The Vampire Hunt   13

CHAPTER FOUR: "Good-bye, Livvy"   17

part two: one month earlier

CHAPTER FIVE: Livvy's Graduation Party   23

CHAPTER SIX: Night Birds   29

part three: earlier that day

CHAPTER SEVEN: The Evil at Home   39

CHAPTER EIGHT: "The Monster Did It"   46

CHAPTER NINE: The Vampire in the Tree   51

CHAPTER TEN: Is Livvy in the House?   55

CHAPTER ELEVEN: Rip   59

part four

CHAPTER TWELVE: Livvy's New Love   71

CHAPTER THIRTEEN: A Surprise Reunion   76

CHAPTER FOURTEEN: The Taste of Night   80

CHAPTER FIFTEEN: "I'm Not Just a Vampire"   84

CHAPTER SIXTEEN: Destiny Flies   87

CHAPTER SEVENTEEN: Trouble at Ari's House   93

CHAPTER EIGHTEEN: Who Is the Next Victim?   102

part five: two weeks later

CHAPTER NINETEEN: "Maybe He's Just What I Need" 111

CHAPTER TWENTY: "Now You Think I'm a Psycho Nut" 119

CHAPTER TWENTY-ONE: Dad Might Kill Livvy 123

CHAPTER TWENTY-TWO: One Evil Dawn 128

CHAPTER TWENTY-THREE: "I Want to Go Back to My Old Life" 134

CHAPTER TWENTY-FOUR: A Death in the Vampire Family 140

CHAPTER TWENTY-FIVE: "It Won't Be Pretty" 144

CHAPTER TWENTY-SIX: "I'd Like to Tear Destiny to Bits" 147

CHAPTER TWENTY-SEVEN: Blood on Her Lips 150

CHAPTER TWENTY-EIGHT: Livvy's Revenge 154

part six

CHAPTER TWENTY-NINE: The Party Crasher 159

CHAPTER THIRTY: Livvy and Harrison 164

CHAPTER THIRTY-ONE: "You're Still Connected to Your Sister" 167

CHAPTER THIRTY-TWO: A Date with a Vampire 171

CHAPTER THIRTY-THREE: Harrison and Livvy 178

CHAPTER THIRTY-FOUR: Destiny and Patrick 182

CHAPTER THIRTY-FIVE: An Evil Creature of the Night 187

CHAPTER THIRTY-SIX: An Unexpected Murder 190

CHAPTER THIRTY-SEVEN: The Real Murderer 197

part seven: night of the full moon

CHAPTER THIRTY-EIGHT: Harrison's Big Date 203

CHAPTER THIRTY-NINE: Destiny Surprises Patrick 207

CHAPTER FORTY: Livvy Surprises Patrick 213

CHAPTER FORTY-ONE: A Vampire Must Die 216

CHAPTER FORTY-TWO: "One Last Kiss . . . Before I Kill You" 219

CHAPTER FORTY-THREE: Thicker Than Blood 223

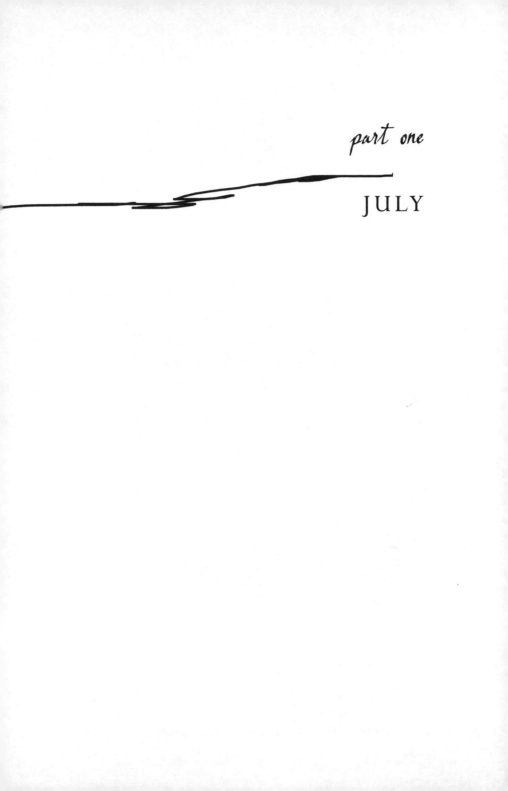

part one

JULY

chapter one

MY SISTER
IS A VAMPIRE

AS DESTINY WELLER MADE THE TURN ONTO COLLINS Drive, a light rain started to fall. She squinted through the windshield, through the tiny, shimmering droplets of water, and pressed her cell phone to her ear.

"I think it's going to get really stormy," she said, glancing up at the lowering, black clouds. "I really don't feel like going out tonight, Ana-Li."

Her friend Ana-Li May made disappointed sounds at the other end. "I know it's hard for you, Dee. But the summer is going fast, you know. You should try to have at least a *little* fun."

Fun? How could she be talking about fun?

Destiny clicked on the headlights. The wipers left a smear on the windshield glass. She kept forgetting to replace the blades.

Hard to think about things like that.

"You've been really great," she told Ana-Li. "I mean, all summer. You're the only one who knows the truth about Livvy. I mean, except for Dad and Mikey. And Ari, of course. And you've been—OH!"

Destiny let out a cry. The cell phone fell from her hand as she hit the brakes hard. Her tiny, silver-gray Civic skidded on the wet pavement.

Startled by the sound, the girl on the sidewalk whipped her head around. Her face came into view.

Destiny gasped. No. Wrong again.

A car honked behind her. Heart pounding, she lowered her foot on the gas pedal and fumbled for the phone.

She could hear Ana-Li on the other end. "What's wrong? Dee? Are you okay?"

"Sorry." She leaned forward to squint through the smeared windshield. The rain pattered down harder. "I keep losing it. Every time I see a girl with long blond hair, I think it's Livvy."

"That's why you've got to get out of yourself," Ana-Li said. "You know. Go out. We'll go to a club or something. Dance our asses off. Maybe meet some hot guys. It'll take your mind off . . . everything."

"How can I take my mind off it?"

She didn't mean to scream, but the words burst out of her in a shrill, trembling voice. "Ana-Li, my twin sister is a *vampire*! She's out flying around, prowling at night, hungry for warm blood, killing—killing things. I . . . I don't know what she's doing. I haven't seen her in two months. Do you know what that's done to my family? To my dad? My poor little brother?"

"Yes, of course I know, Dee. You don't have to scream at me. I—"

"There's *no way* I can take my mind off it," Destiny continued. She made a sharp right, tires skidding again. She'd almost missed her turn. "I think about Livvy all the time. And Ross too. I still can't believe he went with her. Ana-Li, I . . . I want to see Livvy. I just want to hug her. I know it's impossible, but I want to tell her to come back to us."

There was silence at Ana-Li's end.

"Ana-Li? Are you still there?"

"Yeah. I just don't know what to say. You know, I'll be leaving for orientation. Yale is a long way from here. I thought maybe in the short time we have . . ."

Destiny pulled into a parking spot at the curb in front of the familiar, low redbrick building. The rain had slowed. The wipers left a thick, gray smudge as they scraped over the glass.

That's the way I see everything these days, Destiny thought bitterly. Through a dark blur.

"Listen, Ana-Li. I have to go. I'm here, at my dad's office. I have to pick him up because his SUV broke down again. He never takes care of it." She sighed. "He can't seem to take care of anything these days. Just stays in his lab twenty hours a day. Then he comes home too wrecked to talk or do anything."

"Sorry," Ana-Li murmured on the other end.

"No, *I'm* sorry," Destiny said. "Here I am, laying all this on you again for the hundredth time. I'm really sorry. Can I call you later?"

"Yeah. Sure."

She clicked the phone shut and dropped it into her bag. Then she took a deep breath while checking her short, blond hair in the mirror.

Ana-Li has been terrific, she thought. She's always been a great friend. After that horrible night Livvy and Ross decided they wanted to live forever as vampires . . . Ana-Li has always been there for me.

She slid out of the car and gazed up at the sign above the glass door: WELLER VETERINARY CLINIC. Yes, her dad still treated sick cats and dogs, spayed and neutered them, gave them their shots, washed away their fleas, and mended their broken bones. But he spent most of his time in his lab at the back of the building, reading, studying old books, mixing chemicals, working out endless equations, searching for a cure for vampirism.

Destiny made her way through the brightly lit waiting room, empty now, quiet except for the gurgling sounds from the fish tank in the wall. "Hey, Dad—are you ready?" Her voice echoed down the hall as she passed the empty examining rooms.

"Dad?"

She found him hunched over the worktable in the lab, surrounded by darkness, standing under a cone of light from the single ceiling lamp. His eyeglasses reflected the light. He didn't seem to hear her at first.

"Dad? I'm here."

To her surprise, he had tears running down his cheeks. He crumpled the papers in his hand, then furiously ripped them in half and sent them flying to the floor.

"Dad—?"

Dr. Weller turned to Destiny, his face flushed, his eyes hidden behind the shiny glasses. "I'm afraid I have very bad news," he said.

chapter two

"CAN YOU KILL YOUR OWN DAUGHTER?"

DESTINY'S BREATH CAUGHT IN HER THROAT. "DAD—what is it?" she finally choked out. She hurried across the room and stood across the table from him, under the bright, white light.

He shook his head. "It's my work. It's going nowhere. I'm no closer to finding a cure than I was two months ago."

Destiny grabbed the edge of the metal table with both hands. "But you'll keep trying, right, Dad? I mean, you're not giving up, are you?"

His pale blue eyes stared at her from behind his glasses, thick gray eyebrows arching high on his balding head. "I don't know how much time I have." His voice came out in a whisper. His eyes didn't move from Destiny's. "I'm under a lot of pressure."

"Pressure? I don't understand, Dad."

He stepped around the table and put an arm around her shoulders. "A lot of pressure." He hugged her briefly, then guided her to his small office at the side of the lab.

He dropped heavily into his desk chair, brushing back the tuft of gray hair on top of his head. Destiny stood, tense, in front of the desk, arms crossed over the front of her blue T-shirt.

"You know I have chosen two roles," Dr. Weller said, gazing up at her. "I'm the Restorer, the one who can restore neophyte vampires to their normal lives, if they're not already complete vampires."

I know very well, Destiny thought with a shiver. You don't have to explain, Dad. You restored *me*, remember? I was bitten too, just like Livvy. But you restored me, and now I'm fine, perfectly normal. But Livvy . . .

"And I'm also the Hunter," her dad continued, breaking into her thoughts. "Ever since your mother died . . . killed herself because of a vampire . . . I . . . I . . . I've vowed to kill as many vampires as I can. To rid Dark Springs of this . . . this filthy plague."

He rubbed his chin. Destiny saw that he hadn't shaved for at least a day or two. "My two roles . . . curing and hunting . . . they don't always go together."

"What do you mean, Dad? Destiny lowered herself into the wooden armchair across from the desk. "What's going on?"

"I've been working so hard to find a cure," he said. "You

know. A cure for Livvy. And for Ross too. And any other vampire who wants it. And I've been neglecting my duties as a hunter."

Destiny leaned forward, her hands tightly clasped. All her muscles tensed as her father went on.

"The vampires in this town . . . they've become an even bigger danger. There are too many of them. People are starting to become aware . . ."

Destiny swallowed. "You mean, that couple that was murdered in Millerton Woods last weekend?"

Dr. Weller nodded. "The police have been able to keep everything quiet. People in Dark Springs don't know about the vampires. Like your friends, Dee. Your friends all think that Livvy and Ross ran away together. They . . . they don't know the truth."

Destiny nodded. "Just Ana-Li knows. And Ari, because he was there that night. No one else."

Dr. Weller frowned, deep lines creasing his forehead. "Well, people are starting to guess. The police have been getting calls. Mayor Hambrick has been getting frightened calls. He wants to get the governor to call in the National Guard. I can't let that happen. Too many innocent people will be killed."

"What are you going to do?" Destiny asked.

"I have no choice. I have to get my hunters together. I have to hunt them down—and kill as many vampires as I can."

Destiny let out a sharp cry. "Kill them?"

She suddenly pictured Livvy . . . Livvy before this all happened . . . when their mother was still alive. Livvy in that sexy red halter dress she wore to the spring dance their junior year. Her hair all shimmering, cascading down her bare back. The bright red lipstick . . . her sparkly earrings . . . her smile . . .

Destiny shook herself to chase the picture away.

"You can't just go out and kill vampires," she told her father. "How will you find them?"

Dr. Weller leaned forward over the desk. He grabbed Destiny's hands and held them between his. "There's an abandoned apartment building across the river from the campus. It was supposed to be student housing, a dorm for the community college. But the construction company went bankrupt and the building was never finished."

Destiny narrowed her eyes at him. "And—?"

"We think several vampires are using that building. Sleeping there during the day. Living in the apartments. I have my hunters organized. We're going there. Going into those apartments and killing as many of them as we can."

Destiny pulled her hands free. She jumped to her feet. "When? When are you doing this?"

"In two weeks—the next full moon."

Destiny swallowed, her throat suddenly dry. "Two weeks!"

He nodded. "Yes. We'll go in at sunrise when they're all asleep. I wanted to warn you. I mean, if something happens to me . . ." His voice trailed off.

"But, Dad—" Destiny realized she was shaking. "What about Livvy? What if Livvy is in one of those apartments? You . . . you can't kill your own daughter. You can't!"

A sob escaped Dr. Weller's throat. "My daughter is already dead."

Destiny moved around the desk and grabbed her father's sleeve. "But she's not! She's still alive. You know she's not dead. You can't do it. You can't kill her—can you?"

"I don't know!" Dr. Weller hugged Destiny again and held her tight. "I don't know. I don't know! If I find Livvy in there . . . I don't know what I'll do."

chapter three

THE
VAMPIRE HUNT

DR. WELLER PULLED THE DARK BASEBALL CAP DOWN over his head and gazed up at the moon, full and low in the sky, pale white as the sun began to rise. Dressed in black, hats down over their foreheads, the hunters—twenty volunteers—gathered in a silent circle around him at the open entrance to the tall apartment building.

Dr. Weller heard the flap of wings high in the sky. He glanced up the side of the redbrick building, at the window openings, glassless and dark. A tall pile of concrete blocks stood near the front of the entrance. Boards of Sheetrock in varying sizes, wire, and rolls of cable were strewn across the ground. Signs that the construction had stopped abruptly, long before the building had been completed.

A thin arc of red sunlight rose in the distance. The

hunters leaned on their wooden stakes, waiting for their orders.

Dr. Weller took a deep breath. "The vampires should be sleeping by now," he said, eyes raised to the window holes. "But this may not be easy. If they somehow got word that we were coming . . ."

"We can handle them," a young man said, raising his stake in front of him like a knight's lance.

"They might have set a trap for us," Dr. Weller said. "We need to take all precautions. As we spread out in there, we need to be in constant communication. Did you check your walkie-talkies?"

Some of them muttered yes. Some nodded. Some reached for the phones clipped to their belts.

"Make sure they're all set on the same frequency," he continued. "If you're in any trouble, just press the button and shout your location. We'll all hear you."

They nodded again. One man at the edge of the circle made a striking motion with his pointed stake, as if he were killing a vampire.

"Let's go," Dr. Weller said. He hoped they didn't see the shudder that ran down his body. He spun to the building and began jogging toward the entrance, raising his stake as he ran.

Livvy? Ross? Are you in here?

The thought of his daughter lying white and pale, asleep in this vacant building, made his stomach churn. He could feel the muscles tightening in his throat. A wave of nausea swept over him, and for a moment, he thought he was going to vomit.

Livvy?

Oh, Livvy.

Then he was inside the dark lobby, cooler in here, the smell of plywood and pine and plaster dust, and his stomach settled. Through his glasses, his vision grew sharp as he focused his mind. In the dim light, he could see the half-tiled walls, the opening of the elevator shaft.

He suddenly could hear every footstep of his hunters, hear their shallow breaths, even hear their *thoughts*! At least, he imagined he could.

Every sense alive now.

Alive. Yes, I want to stay alive. I don't want to die tonight in a nest of vampires.

A nest of the *undead*.

Undead. My own daughter . . .

A shaft of red sunlight poured through the open lobby windows. The day was pushing out the night. He felt as if he were moving through a dream, colors changing, darkness giving way to bright light.

Trying to force away all thoughts, he led the hunters to the stairs. And as they climbed, single file up the concrete stairway, shoes thudding and scraping the dust, Dr. Weller heard the moans. Soft at first, then louder as they stepped out onto the first floor.

A shrill animal howl somewhere down the long hall-way. Open doorways to the left.

Stakes gripped against their sides, the hunters trotted toward the open doorways. Dr. Weller clicked on his flashlight and sent a beam ahead of them on the floor. He saw piles of trash, rattling and blowing from the gusts of wind through the glassless windows.

Sudden movement. An animal scampered out from under the trash. Dr. Weller stopped and motioned for his hunters to stay back, and then lowered the beam of yellow light to the creature. A fat raccoon.

The animal waddled away from the light, down the trash-cluttered hall, followed by four small raccoons, running hard to keep up.

Dr. Weller motioned for his posse to move again. Stepping over the garbage and stacks of newspaper, they walked silently toward the dark apartments.

No doors on the apartments. They heard hoarse coughs. Loud snoring. Eerie moans and groans . . .

Yes, they're here.

Yes, they're asleep.

Yes, it's time.

Dr. Weller raised his wooden stake and pointed it down the hall. "Let's kill vampires!" he cried.

chapter four

"GOOD-BYE, LIVVY"

HE STEPPED INTO THE FIRST APARTMENT, WOODEN stake raised in his right hand, flashlight gripped in his left. He swept the light around the floor. It stopped on a figure sprawled on his back, arms dangling over a nearly flat mattress on the floor.

Heart pounding, Dr. Weller moved closer. A young man, asleep, his mouth open. And the dark stain on his chin . . . the dark stain . . . caked blood. Running down his chin onto his bare chest.

He must die. I have no choice. I have accepted this responsibility.

But yet Dr. Weller hesitated. Am I taking a human life? No.

Not human. Not human any longer.

A scream of agony ended his thought, followed by another shrill scream from down the hall. The hunters had found their prey. Vampires were being slaughtered.

He set down the flashlight. He raised the pointed stake high in both hands.

Another scream of horror from another apartment.

The young man stirred in his sleep. Closed his mouth. Eyes still shut, he licked at the caked blood on his chin.

With a loud grunt, Dr. Weller arched the stake high, then brought it down with all his force. The point pierced the young man's chest, then sank deep into his body.

His arms shot up and his legs kicked. He opened his eyes wide and a scream of pain shattered the silence of the room.

Dr. Weller buried the stake deeper, pushing hard, gripping it with both hands. The vampire's eyes sank into their sockets. The arms and legs, still now, began to shrink. A rush of air escaped the vampire's mouth, and then he didn't move again.

Dr. Weller freed the stake with a sharp tug. It pulled out easily, no blood on the tip.

He grabbed the flashlight and lurched back out into the hall. Screams echoed off the plaster walls. Screams and howls of pain and shock, and the hard-running footsteps of the hunters as they invaded the open apartments to kill their deadly prey.

Dr. Weller stopped for a moment to catch his breath. Then he dove into the next apartment, the wooden stake trembling in his hand.

The light danced over the apartment floor. A small, square rug in one corner. A suitcase against the wall. A wooden table cluttered with bottles and tubes and jars of cosmetics.

Dr. Weller swallowed. A female vampire lived here. His legs suddenly felt weak as he moved toward the bedroom in back. The flashlight grew heavy in his hand. He took a deep breath. Held it. Burst into the room.

And saw her sleeping on a low cot.

He recognized her with his first glance. Livvy.

Oh, no. Livvy.

She had cut her hair as short as Destiny's. She wore a long, black nightshirt down over her knees. Her hands were crossed over her chest. In the trembling glow of the flashlight, her short, blond hair shimmered around her pale, sleeping face.

I can't do this, he thought.

I brought her into the world. How can I kill her now? I despise all vampires. A vampire murdered my wife, took away the person most precious to me.

I hate them. Hate them all.

But to drive a stake through my own daughter? That's asking too much of any man.

Images flashed through his mind, bright and clear as photographs. Livvy as a baby. Livvy and Destiny in their snowsuits building their first snowman. Livvy and her mom giving each other makeovers, bright purple lipstick shining on his wife's lips, sparkles in her hair.

Livvy . . .

I can't.

With a sob, he turned to leave. He stopped when she stirred, groaning in her sleep.

She's not my daughter, he realized.

It's not Livvy anymore. It's a deadly creature in Livvy's body. And I have no choice.

He moved back to the cot. Raised the stake high in both hands. Changed his mind.

One last kiss for my daughter. A good-bye kiss.

Good-bye, Livvy.

He lowered his face to her cheek.

And he let out a startled cry as her hands shot up. Her eyes opened wide. She grabbed him by the neck and tightened her fingers around his throat.

"Ohh—" he gasped.

She stared up at him, and the fingers squeezed tighter, tighter . . .

"NO!" he choked out, struggling to free himself from her grip. "NO! LIVVY—PLEASE! NO!"

part two

ONE MONTH
EARLIER

chapter five

LIVVY'S
GRADUATION PARTY

"I LOVE THE BLUE EYE SHADOW. IT'S SO RETRO," Livvy said. She turned to her two new friends, Suzie and Monica. "How does it look?"

"Awesome," Suzie said. "But wait. You have lipstick on your chin." She dabbed a tissue over the dark spot on Livvy's chin. "There."

"Is that the cinnamon lipstick or the grape?" Monica asked. She shoved Suzie aside to get a better look at Livvy. "It's so hard to tell in this light."

A single sixty-watt bulb hung on a long cord from the ceiling.

Livvy took the tissue from Suzie and dabbed at her lips. "It's black. For nighttime. My favorite time."

Monica grinned at Livvy. "My favorite time too. Party

time." She licked her full, dark lips. Then she picked up her hairbrush and began running it through her long, straight black hair.

"Hey, it's date night," Suzie said.

"Every night is date night," Monica said, "when you're hungry."

Livvy turned to Suzie. "Are you coming with us?"

"I think we should go out on our own," Suzie replied. "See what's out there. Check out the fresh meat. You know. And then we can meet later."

Livvy studied Suzie's face, so pale, nearly white as snow. Suzie had been an immortal for a long time, for so long Suzie didn't remember when she made the change.

One night when the moon was still high in the sky, and the three girls had fed well and were feeling comfortable and full, Suzie told Livvy and Monica her story. She'd had a tough time, chased from town to town, nearly caught by vampire hunters in a city near Dark Springs.

Her troubles showed on her face, Livvy thought. Suzie's pale, papery skin was pulled tight against her skull, so tight her cheekbones nearly poked out. Her hair was patchy and thin. Her arms were as skinny as broom handles, her fingers bony, almost skeletal. Her eyes had started to sink back into their sockets.

She tried to cover it up with loads of makeup and by wearing trendy clothes, young people's clothes. And she stayed in the darkest corners of the night, swooping out only when prey was near. But Suzie was too far gone to hide the fact that she was an immortal.

That won't happen to me, Livvy thought. I won't that happen to me.

Livvy tossed back her blond hair with a shake of her head. She had cut it short—short as her sister's—and she loved the way it felt now, light as a breeze. "Wish we had a mirror," she murmured.

Suzie laughed. "What good would that do? We don't have reflections, remember?"

The lightbulb over their heads flickered and went out. Livvy sighed. "The generator must have conked out again."

Some clever immortals had hooked up a power generator to the building across the street. The stolen electricity provided light for the whole building. But the generator was too small and kept blowing out.

"Wish we lived in a fancy hotel," Monica said, still brushing her hair. "Instead of this empty apartment building. We could send down for room service. You know. Dial the phone and say, 'Just send the waiter up. We don't need any food.'"

Livvy laughed. "Forget room service. I just want to live in a place where the lights stay on."

"Lights hurt my eyes," Suzie complained, furiously powdering her face.

"I don't mean *bright* lights," Livvy said. "None of us can stand *bright* lights. I just mean lights that don't flicker on and off every few minutes."

The three new friends had built their dressing table out

of plywood and concrete blocks left by the builders of the unfinished building. They had set it up in front of the glassless window where they could sit and watch the sunset.

Livvy had found a cot in one of the downstairs rooms and dragged it up to her bedroom. Suzie and Monica shared an apartment downstairs but came to Livvy's room in the evening to do their makeup and get ready to go out.

Livvy liked them both. Monica was big and dark and sexy and had no trouble getting the guys. And Suzie had the experience. She knew everything they needed to know to survive.

"When's the full moon?" Monica asked, adjusting the top of her tank top.

"I think it's in a few weeks," Suzie said, gazing up at the darkening sky. A faint smile crossed her pale lips. "Warm blood under a bright full moon. Poetry, right? Does it get any better than that? I don't think so."

Livvy turned to her. "What about tonight? They'll be some hot guys out tonight. Why wait?"

Monica brushed her arm. "Hey, didn't they have graduation at your school this morning? I thought I saw some cute guys walking around in blue robes."

Livvy glared at her. "Why bring that up?"

Monica backed away. "Whoa. I didn't mean anything. I was just asking."

"Do I give a damn about high school graduation?" Livvy snapped. She surprised herself at how angry she felt. Was she angry at Monica—or at something else? "I don't give a damn. Trust me."

"Okay, okay." Monica raised both hands as if asking for a truce.

"I've already graduated," Livvy said, still feeling upset. "I've graduated to what I want to be." She stood up. "Hey, maybe tonight I'll celebrate my graduation. Maybe I'll have a little graduation party of my own."

"We'll all party tonight!" Monica said, licking her lips.

Suzie gazed out the window. She seemed to be in her own world. "You know," she said, finally turning back to them, "the better looking the boy, the richer the blood."

"No way," Monica insisted. "That's superstition."

"It's a proven fact," Suzie said, toying with a strand of her long hair.

"Who proved it?" Livvy asked.

"I did." Suzie grinned. "Listen to me. The hot guys have the hottest blood."

Monica stared at her. "No lie?"

"No lie."

Livvy sighed. "I get so high when the blood is fresh and warm. I mean . . . the way it feels on my lips and then on my tongue. I can feel it all the way down my throat. And afterwards, it's so wild. I always feel like I'm flying . . . just flying out of my body, into outer space."

"I always feel so warm," Suzie said, her eyes dreamy. She sighed. "Like a happy, contented baby. But then the hunger starts again. So soon . . . it starts again, that gnawing . . . that needy feeling."

"Let's keep it light," Livvy scolded. "It's my graduation

party tonight, remember?" She stood up. "How do I look?"

She had her short, shimmery hair combed straight back, pale lip gloss, light blue eye shadow covering her eyelids, a pink midriff top over low-riding, white jeans, lots of bare skin showing, three earrings in each ear, a glittery rhinestone in her right nostril.

She walked up and down the bare room, doing the model strut. Monica and Suzie made admiring sounds. "Whoa. I love the nighttime!" Livvy exclaimed. "I feel lucky tonight!"

She realized that Suzie was staring past her. "Hey, what's up?"

She turned—and saw a fat brown field mouse hunched near the open doorway, gazing up at them with its shiny black marble eyes.

Suzie spun off her chair and lowered her lean body into a crouch, eyes unblinking, locked on the mouse.

"Oh, no. You wouldn't," Livvy said. "It's so cute."

With a sudden lightning movement, Suzie pounced. The mouse let out a squeak as Suzie grabbed it, wrapped her fingers around its stubby brown fur.

Its last squeak.

Suzie tore off its head and tossed it out into the hall. Then she tilted the body over her mouth and squeezed out the juice.

When she had finished, dark blood trickling down her chin, she heaved the drained corpse into the hall. Then she turned to Livvy and Monica with a grin. "Appetizer," she whispered.

chapter six

NIGHT
BIRDS

LIVVY TRANSFORMED INTO A SLENDER BLACKBIRD. She perched on the windowsill, gazing out at the purple night sky.

Her feathers felt stiff and scratchy, and it took a while to get used to the rapid pattering of her heart. Once she adjusted to seeing two views at once, her eyesight was sharp.

She raised her wings and lifted off the window. The cool air ruffled her chest feathers. She swooped higher, pale white stars blinking so close above her. What a thrill!

To fly. To be free of the ground. To swoop and soar like a wild creature.

I'll never get tired of this, Livvy thought.

And then she felt the hunger, a sharp pang that tightened her belly. She opened her beak and let the onrushing air cool her throat. The gnawing hunger was insistent, wave after wave, until she felt dizzy from the need.

I have to feed.

What will I find tonight? Who will help me quench my thirst?

The yellow moon loomed above her, wisps of gray cloud snaking across it. Livvy lifted her wings and floated, gazing up at the moonlight.

No one else can see the moon like this. I am so lucky.

But then she felt a ripple in the wind at her side and heard the flutter of wings. Livvy turned and saw another blackbird, more plump with a streak of white in its wings, soar beside her.

The two blackbirds flew together, side by side, wings touching. They lifted high toward the stars, then shot low above the shimmering trees.

Livvy landed softly in tall grass and felt the dew tickle her feathers. The other bird shook its wings hard as it bounced to a landing a few feet beside her.

They both transformed quickly into their human forms.

Straightening her pink top, Livvy gazed at Ross Starr. The moonlight gave his short, blond hair a glow. He wore straight-legged jeans and a sleeveless T-shirt that showed off his muscular arms. He flashed her his Hollywood smile— the smile that had convinced her she needed Ross, needed to bring him with her to the other side.

"Hey, Ross," she murmured. "What's up? That was nice, wasn't it."

He stepped forward and kissed her. "You and me. Flying together. Yeah. That's what it's about, right?"

He tried to hug her, but Livvy pulled away. "I'm hungry. I mean, I'm starving." She held her stomach. "I . . . can't even think straight."

He smiled again. "Oh, yeah. Fresh nectar. I want mine super-sized!"

She kissed him on the cheek. "Get lost, okay?"

He grabbed her around the waist and pulled her to him. "Come on, Liv. I need more than a kiss. You look so hot tonight."

"Ross, please—" She squeezed his hands, then pushed them off her. "I told you I need to feed."

He shrugged. "Okay. I'll come with you."

"Oh, sure. That'll be helpful. You're gonna help me pick up a guy?"

He frowned at her. "I don't like you with other guys."

"What's your problem? He's not a guy. He's a meal."

She didn't hear what he said next. She transformed quickly, stretching her wings, ruffling the stiff tail feathers, a blackbird again.

She bent her thin bird legs, pushed up from the dew-wet grass, letting her wings lift her . . . lift her . . . over the treetops. She saw Ross swoop ahead of her, then fall back, teasing her, following her despite her pleas.

He bumped her playfully, swiped his beak against her side, lowered his head and bumped her again.

They flew side by side, gliding over Millerton Woods,

light and shadows over the thick tangle of trees, shivering under the golden moonlight.

Livvy made a wide turn, wings straight out at her sides, and realized she was flying over Collins Drive now. Her father's office came into view. The light glowed from the front window. Was he still at work this late at night?

She swooped higher, away from the little, brick building. I don't want to see him. He's not part of my life anymore.

Flying low, the two blackbirds turned onto Main Street. Livvy landed behind a maple tree and gazed at the people in line at the movie theater. Ross dropped beside her.

They transformed into their human shapes, hidden by the thick tree trunk.

"You know, graduation was this morning," Ross said.

"Shut up," Livvy replied sharply.

"How are we going to get jobs?" Ross said. "We're not high school graduates."

"You're so funny," Livvy replied. "Not."

Ross turned to the movie theater. "What's playing? A vampire movie?"

Livvy's stomach growled. She ignored Ross and his jokes. I've never fed in a movie theater, she thought. It's dark enough—and the sound is loud enough to muffle the scream.

Livvy's victims only screamed once. They always screamed at the first bite, then gave in to the pleasure.

"Oh, no. Oh, wow." A moan escaped Ross's throat.

Livvy turned from the faces in the movie line. "What's wrong?"

He leaned forward, peering around the tree trunk. "My family is there. See them? Mom and Dad and Emily."

Livvy saw Ross's sister first, then his parents. "Don't worry. They can't see us."

"I . . . I want to see them," Ross said. "Livvy, I'd just like to talk to them for a little while. You know. See how Emily is doing and everything. They think I ran away with you. I want to tell them I'm okay."

"Ross, you can't," Livvy said. "You know you can't do that. You'll only upset them. You'll mess them up even worse."

"But—I just want to say hi," Ross said. "I guess I'm homesick."

"It won't work. Trust me." Livvy stared hard at him. She could see how excited and upset he was.

"Maybe I feel homesick too. But listen to me. I made a vow," Livvy told him. "I vowed I'd never go back home. You need to make the same vow. It's not our world anymore. We've chosen a different world. You know. A more exciting life. I . . . I'm not going to torture myself by trying to drop in on Destiny and Dad and . . . and . . ."

She couldn't say Mikey's name. Thinking about Mikey always made her cry.

"I guess you're right," Ross said. "But look. My family— they're going inside the theater. I could just walk over, say hi, and leave."

"No. Go away, Ross. Fly away—now. You know I'm right."

Sighing, he watched until his family disappeared inside. Then he kissed Livvy on the cheek. "Later."

He changed quickly. Raised his wings and fluttered off the ground. She watched him hover over the sidewalk. Then she changed into a blackbird too, turned and flew away.

I don't want to hear about how homesick Ross is, she thought. A shudder ran down her body. The air suddenly felt cold. The moonlight sent down no warmth.

I shouldn't have brought Ross to this new life. I care about him. I still do. Maybe not like before. But I care about him.

But he's too sentimental. He's too soft.

I thought he was strong, but he isn't. He always seemed so confident. I can still see him with that strutting walk of his, moving down the halls at school, flashing that great smile. I used to wait for him to come by. I had such a major crush on him.

But now . . . he's weak. His attitude is wrong. He's not thinking right.

He'll get himself killed. I know he will.

Hunger gnawed at her, interrupting her thoughts. She glanced down and saw flashing lights on a big, square building.

Where am I?

Sliding on a wind current, she let herself down and recognized the dance club: Rip.

Oh, yes. Lots of fresh talent here. Kids hanging out in the dimly lit parking lot. Lined up at the entrance. Lots of dark corners, and the woods close behind the parking lot.

Lots of older guys getting trashed at the bar and looking to hook up.

How perfect is that for a hungry vampire?

And there below her she saw Suzie and Monica at the entrance, chatting with two guys, about to go in.

Excellent.

Livvy dropped to the gravel path at the side of the building. She could hear the throbbing beats from inside, hear laughing voices, the roar of a crowd.

Yes, yes, yes. I'm so hungry.

I'm sure some lucky guy will be happy to come to the woods with me.

She transformed into her human body, brushed a few feathers off the front of her jeans, tugged down the top of her top to look sexier—and hurried to meet her friends.

part three

EARLIER
THAT DAY

chapter seven

THE EVIL
AT HOME

"AS YOU LEAVE THIS HIGH SCHOOL WHERE YOU HAVE spent four wonderful years of growth and learning . . . As you go forth into the world—no longer students—you must realize that the world belongs to you now. Your generation will decide where we all go next. You will be the ones to shape the future. You will be the ones . . ."

Destiny tuned out as the graduation speaker droned on. She wiped her sweaty hands in the folds of her blue robe.

"It's so hot in here," she whispered to the girl next to her. "When can we take these things off?"

The flat blue cap, tilted over her head, felt as if it weighed a hundred pounds. Destiny knew it was going to leave a permanent dent in her hair. Sweat streamed down her forehead. Would the cap leave a blue stain on her skin?

She glanced at the rows of robed kids on the stage. As they all gathered in the auditorium this morning, her friends had been bursting with excitement about graduation. Ana-Li May was practically *flying*, swirling around in circles, making her graduation robe whirl around her.

Fletch Green, Ross's best friend, gave Destiny such a big hug, he accidentally knocked her cap off her head. "Do you believe I graduated in only four years?" he exclaimed. "My parents predicted six!"

Ari Stark seemed excited too. He greeted her with a kiss. "Freedom!" he shouted. "A few more hours, and we're *outta* here! Freedom! Freedom!" He started a chant, and a few other kids joined in.

A sad smile crossed Destiny's face. She knew why her friends were so happy and excited. They really were getting out of here, out of Dark Springs. They were going away to college. In a few months Ari would be at Princeton in New Jersey. And Ana-Li would be off at Yale being brilliant the way she always was.

And I'll be here, Destiny thought, unable to fight away her sadness. I was accepted at four schools, including Dartmouth, where I really wanted to go. But no. I'll be here, living at home, going to the dinky Community College.

But what choice did I have? How could I leave Mikey, my poor, troubled little brother? How could I leave Dad? They both need me so much now . . . now that Livvy . . .

She wanted to be excited and happy. Graduating from high school was a major thing in your life. It was supposed to be a day you'd never forget.

And it *was* kind of thrilling to march slowly down the auditorium aisle in time to "Pomp and Circumstance," the music played at every graduation. And to hear your name called, and walk up to receive your diploma.

Destiny smiled and waved the diploma at her dad. She could see him wave back to her from the fourth row.

Kind of exciting.

But then the kids in her class settled into their folding chairs, sweating under their robes, shifting the caps on their heads. And the balding, scratchy-voiced speaker in his tight-fitting gray suit—an assistant mayor, she thought—began to speak.

". . . The future isn't only a promise, it's a responsibility. How will you find your role in the future? By looking to the past. Because the past is where our future springs from . . ."

Yawn.

As he rambled on, his voice faded from Destiny's ears. And she felt the sadness rise over her, like a powerful ocean wave.

There should be an empty seat next to me, she thought. A chair for Livvy. Livvy would have been here with me this morning, and we would have been so happy.

Destiny gazed down the rows of blue-robed kids. And there should be a chair for Ross. Destiny felt a flash of anger. Yes, I had a crush on Ross—and Livvy knew it. And she took him away . . . where no one will ever see him again. So selfish . . . so stupid and selfish . . .

There should be a chair here for Ross. He should be

graduating today. And there should be two more empty chairs, Destiny thought. Chairs for our friends, Courtney and Bree, both murdered by vampires.

Four empty chairs. Four kids who will not graduate this morning.

The sadness was overwhelming. Destiny felt hot tears streaming down her cheeks. She turned her head away. She didn't want her father to see.

Poor Dad. He must be thinking the same things, she told herself. Somehow he's managing to keep it together. I have to try hard to keep it together too. She glanced down at the red leather cover on her diploma and saw that it was stained by her tears.

Loud cheers startled Destiny from her thoughts. All around her, kids leaped up and tossed their caps in the air. Blinking away her sadness, Destiny climbed to her feet and tossed her cap too.

The ceremony had ended. I'm a high school graduate, she thought. I've spent twelve years with most of these kids. And now we're all going to scatter and start new lives.

New lives . . .

She couldn't stop thinking about Livvy. No way to shut her out of her mind, even for a few minutes.

"Return your robes to the gym, people," Mr. Farrow, the principal, boomed over the loudspeaker. "Don't forget to return your robes to the gym."

All around her, kids were hugging, laughing, talking excitedly. Some jumped off the stage and ran up the auditorium aisles to meet their parents.

She waved to Ari, hurried to return her robe, then found her dad outside in front of the school talking to some other parents.

It was a warm June morning, the sun already high in a clear blue sky. Yellow lilies circling the flagpole waved gently in a warm breeze. Families filled the front lawn of the school, snapping photos, chatting, and laughing.

Dr. Weller turned when he saw Destiny and wrapped her in a big hug. "Congratulations," he said. She saw the tears in his eyes. She hugged him again.

"We have to make this a happy day," he said. "We really have to try, don't we?"

Destiny nodded. Her chin trembled. She fought off the urge to cry.

"I have to get to my office," Dr. Weller said. "But I'll take you and Mikey out for dinner tonight—our own private celebration. Good?"

"Good," she replied. She saw Ari and Ana-Li come out of the building.

"If Ari would like to come with us tonight . . ." her dad started. He had grown used to seeing Ari around the house at all hours. The two of them got along pretty well.

"I think he's going out with his family," Destiny said.

Dr. Weller nodded. "The three of us. We'll have a nice dinner." She walked him to his SUV. It took him four tries to start it up.

"Dad, you've really got to get this car serviced," Destiny said.

He smiled at her. "It's on my list."

"Dad, you know you don't *have* a list."

"It's on my list to make a list." Tires squealing, he pulled away.

Destiny felt a tap on her shoulder. She turned and Ari kissed her. "Hey, we're graduates. I'm totally psyched. Do you believe it? No more gym class. No more Coach Green telling me what a loser I am."

Ana-Li laughed. "Just because you have a diploma doesn't mean you're not a loser."

Ari pretended to be hurt. "What's up with that? You're dissing me on graduation day?"

Ana-Li opened her diploma and held it up. "Check it out. They misspelled my name. Two n's."

"That's terrible," Destiny said, studying the diploma. "How could they do that?"

"It means you didn't really graduate," Ari told Ana-Li. "No one will believe that's your diploma. Your whole life is going to be messed up now."

Ana-Li shook her tiny fist at Ari. "I'm going to mess *you* up!"

Laughing, Ari raised both fists and began dancing from side to side. "You want a piece of me? Huh? You want a piece of me?"

Ana-Li ignored him. She turned to Destiny. "How you doing?"

"Tough morning," Destiny replied. "You know."

Ari lowered his fists. His smile faded.

"What are you two doing now?" Destiny asked. "Want

to come back with me? We can sit around and reminisce or something."

"Is lunch included in this invitation?" Ari asked.

Destiny nodded.

"Count me in."

"Just let me say good-bye to my parents, and I'll meet you at your house," Ana-Li said. She trotted back toward the school.

Ari slid an arm over Destiny's shoulders, and they walked the few blocks to her house. Cars filled with their friends rolled by, horns honking, music blaring from open windows.

"Did you hear about Fletch's party last night?" Ari asked. "His parents were in L.A. So Fletch had two kegs. Everyone got trashed. And his brother's garage band played all night."

Destiny sighed. "I'm sorry. I know you wanted to go. But I just didn't feel like partying."

They stepped onto her front stoop. Destiny fumbled in her bag for her key. She found it, turned the key in the lock, pushed open the front door—and screamed.

"OH, NO!"

Ari grabbed her and they both stared in disbelief at the living room walls.

Fanged creatures with curled horns on their heads . . . A winged, two-headed demon, both heads spewing black blood . . . A grinning devil . . .

Ugly, black demons painted all over the walls.

chapter eight

"THE MONSTER DID IT"

"OH, NO! OH, NO!" DESTINY HELD ONTO ARI AND pressed her head against his shoulder. Staring at the crude, childish paintings, she led the way into the house.

"This is too weird," Ari muttered.

Destiny opened her mouth to speak. But a shrill cry interrupted her—and Mikey came leaping off the stairs onto Ari's shoulders. He curled his hands around Ari's throat and screamed, "I'm a MONSTER! I'll kill you! I'll KILL you!"

Ari dropped to the floor under the eight-year-old boy's weight. He sprawled on his back and pried Mikey's fingers from around his neck. "Whoa. Easy, man. Mikey, you're choking me."

"I'm not Mikey. I'm a *monster!*"

Destiny reached down to help pull Mikey off.

"Hey, what's up?" Ana-Li burst into the room. She let out a cry when she saw the crude creatures smeared over walls. "Ohmigod."

Destiny pulled Mikey to his feet, then tugged him away from Ari. "Calm down. Don't move. Just take a deep breath, okay?"

Mikey tossed back his head and let out a hoarse, demonic laugh.

Destiny kept a hand on his thick, coppery hair, holding him in place. Mikey was slender and light, small for eight, with arms and legs like sticks. He had dark, serious eyes that looked as if they belonged on an adult. His front teeth were crooked because he refused to wear his retainer.

Groaning, Ari climbed to his feet. Ana-Li couldn't take her eyes off the walls.

"I can't believe you did this," Destiny said, shaking her head.

"I *told* you I didn't do it. The monster did it," Mikey insisted, finally back in his normal, high-pitched voice.

Destiny and Ana-Li exchanged glances. Ana-Li knew the problems they'd been having with Mikey. The poor kid had been acting out, severely troubled by the loss of his sister.

He had nightmares that made him scream. He was afraid to stand near an open window. He'd been getting into fights at school. Sometimes he was afraid of the dark. But he kept his room dark as a cave and spent hour after hour in there with the door locked.

Destiny never knew what to expect. Sometimes Mikey acted like a terrified victim, trembling, crying. And other times, he acted like a monster, striking out, screaming in a rage.

She felt so bad for the little guy . . . and so totally helpless.

Ari stepped up to the wall and examined the paintings. "I think the monster is in trouble big-time," he said to Mikey. "How do you think the monster should be punished?"

"His head should be cut off with a machete," Mikey answered. "And then they should turn him upside down and let all his blood drain out on the floor."

Ari turned to Destiny. "Big trouble," he whispered.

"Wasn't anyone here watching Mikey?" Ana-Li asked.

Destiny sighed. She turned to Mikey. "Where is Mrs. Miller? She was supposed to watch you."

"She had to go home to check something," Mikey said. "She didn't come back. I guess she got busy."

"Mikey's the one who got busy," Ari said, gesturing to the wall.

Mikey let out a roar. His eyes grew wide. "*The monster is coming back,*" he whispered.

"We should get him out in the sunshine for a while," Ana-Li whispered to Destiny. "You know. Take his mind off this stuff."

Destiny nodded. "Hey, how about a soccer game?" she

asked Mikey. "You and me against Ari and Ana-Li."

Mikey reluctantly agreed. Destiny grabbed a soccer ball in the garage and led the way to the backyard, and the four of them started a game.

The Wellers' backyard was deep and wide, covered by a carpet of low grass and interrupted by only a few sycamore and birch trees. Almost perfect for soccer.

The wind had picked up, but the sun blazed high in the sky, making the air warm as summer. Destiny passed the ball to Mikey, and they drove down the field toward Ana-Li and Ari. Mikey brought the ball close to the two slender saplings that formed the goal. Ari made an attempt to block his shot. But Mikey sent the ball flying through the trees. *Goal!*

It was obvious to Destiny that her two friends were letting Mikey be a star. But Mikey didn't notice. He jumped up and down cheering for himself.

This was a good idea, Destiny thought. His mood has changed completely. A little sunshine and some physical exercise, and he's acting like a normal kid again.

The game went well for another ten minutes. Destiny loved the intense expression on her brother's face as he moved the ball forward, dodged Ana-Li and Ari and their feeble attempts to block him, and kicked two more goals.

Destiny began to feel hungry. Maybe it was time to stop the game and make lunch. She looked up in time to see Ari give the ball a hard kick that sent it flying toward the trees at the edge of the yard.

Mikey and Ari both took off after the ball. It hit the trunk of an old sycamore tree hard and bounced off. Mikey slid under the tree, chasing the ball.

Destiny heard a cracking sound. She raised her eyes in time to see a high branch of the tree come crashing down.

"Mikey—look out!" she screamed.

chapter nine

THE VAMPIRE
IN THE TREE

MIKEY'S EYES WENT WIDE.

Destiny heard the crack of branches as the falling limb smashed through them.

Mikey let out a scream, dropped to the ground, and rolled away.

The limb hit the ground a foot or so from Mikey, bounced once, and came to a rest on the grass.

Destiny had her hands pressed to the sides of her face. "Are you okay?" she screamed.

Mikey didn't answer. He jumped to his feet and pointed up to the tree. "Vampire!" he cried. "It's a vampire! In the tree!"

"No, wait—" Ari shouted. He made a grab for Mikey. But Mikey took off, running to the house.

"Mikey, it was just a tree branch," Destiny called. She chased after her brother and caught him at the kitchen door.

"Let go!" he screamed. "It's a vampire. In the tree! Didn't you see it? Didn't you?"

"No. There's nothing up there," Destiny insisted, holding him by the arm. "Listen to me—"

But he jerked his arm free and dove into the house. She heard him sobbing loudly as he scrambled up the stairs to his room.

"Mikey, wait. Please—" Destiny darted up the stairs after him.

He slammed the door in her face. She heard the lock click. She could hear him still sobbing on the other side of the door.

Destiny turned and saw Ari and Ana-Li at the bottom of the stairs. They gazed up at her, their faces tight with concern.

She made her way down the stairs slowly, feeling shaky and upset. "I'd better call Dr. Fishman," she said. "He's Mikey's shrink. He keeps telling us it will just take time. But I've never seen Mikey this bad."

"The poor guy is scared to death," Ari said, shaking his head.

"He sees vampires everywhere," Destiny whispered. "And then sometimes he pretends *he's* a vampire." She led them into the living room. She motioned to the couches, but no one sat down. They stood tensely near the wall.

"I know the only thing that will help him," Destiny said. "Bring Livvy back. He knows the truth about her. Maybe it was a mistake to tell him. He's so scared now. If I could just bring her back here—"

"Hey, I'm scared too," Ana-Li said, hugging herself tightly. She shuddered. "I mean, Livvy and Ross are out there somewhere, right?"

Destiny nodded.

"And they're full vampires now. I mean, real ones. Needy . . . thirsty." She shuddered again.

Ari raised his eyes toward the ceiling. "Shhh. Not so loud. We don't need to be talking about this in front of Mikey."

"But what if they come back here?" Ana-Li whispered. "What if they're out flying around one night, and they're real thirsty? I mean, so thirsty they can't control themselves. And they fly back here and find us? I mean, they could attack us, right? Aren't we obvious victims here?"

"No way," Destiny replied, shaking her head. "She's still my sister. No way she'd come back here and attack my friends." She frowned at Ana-Li. "Do you honestly think Livvy would come back here and drink your blood?"

"I . . . don't know," Ana-Li replied, her voice cracking. "I really don't."

Destiny opened her mouth to reply, but a sudden noise above her head made her stop.

A flapping sound. Like a window shade flapping in a strong wind.

Destiny raised her eyes to the sound and saw a darting, black shadow.

"Hey—!" Ari let out a cry, his mouth open in surprise.

The shadow swooped low.

Destiny felt a cold whoosh of air sweep past the back of her neck.

It took her a while to recognize the sound—the flapping of wings.

And then she saw the bat. Eyes glowing, it soared beneath the dark wood ceiling beams. Then low over their heads, flapping up to the mirror, turning and shooting over them to the other wall. Then flying over them again, lower each time, raising its talons as if preparing to attack.

Ana-Li covered her head. Ari ducked. Destiny opened her mouth in a scream of horror.

chapter ten

IS LIVVY
IN THE HOUSE?

THE BAT LET OUT A SCREECH AND SOARED UP TO THE ceiling. Destiny watched it cling to a beam, wings flapping hard. Its glowing eyes locked on Destiny.

"How did it get in?" Ana-Li cried, clinging to Ari's arm. "What's it doing in here?"

Trembling, Destiny stared up at it. "Livvy? Is that you?" she called, but she could only manage a whisper. "Livvy—?"

And then without warning, the creature let go of the wooden beam and came swooping down.

Destiny saw the eyes glow brighter. Saw the creature raise its talons and arch its wings high behind its ratlike head.

She tried to duck away, bumping hard into Ari and Ana-Li, sending them tumbling against the couch.

Then with another whistling shriek, the bat latched onto Destiny. Wings flapping loudly, it dug its talons into her hair. She heard its ugly cry as she struggled to slap it off.

"*Eeeeee eeeeeeee!*" Like a car alarm going off in her head.

"No! Get off! Get OFF me!"

The talons dug into her scalp. Sharp, stabbing pain swept through her head.

"NO!"

Her heart pounding, Destiny ducked low again, swung her hand, hit the creature hard. She felt its furry warmth. Felt the breeze from its flapping wings, felt the bat's hot breath prickle the back of her neck.

"Get OFF!"

Another hard slap sent the creature sailing to the floor.

Ari raised his foot to stomp on it.

"No—don't!" Destiny screamed, shoving him back.

The bat recovered quickly. It let out a low buzz, then shot back up into the air. Destiny covered her hair with both arms as it swooped low over her again. Then the creature made a sharp turn and flew into the back hallway.

Holding her head, Destiny lurched after it. "Livvy—?" she called. "Is that you?"

The bat darted out the open kitchen window, leaving the yellow window curtains fluttering behind it.

"Oh, wow." Destiny sank onto a white bench at the kitchen table. She brushed back her hair, waiting for her heartbeats to slow.

"Are you okay?" Ari put a hand on her shoulder. "Dee, you're shaking."

"It . . . attacked me," she stammered. "Why did it attack me?"

Ana-Li opened the refrigerator and pulled out a bottle of water. She spun off the top and handed it to Destiny. "Here. Drink something. Try to calm down. You're okay, right?"

Destiny nodded. She took a long drink of the cold water.

Then she turned back to her friends. "Why would a bat fly into the house in the middle of the day? And why did it attack me?"

Ari shrugged. Ana-Li stared back at Destiny without an answer.

Destiny took another drink. "How can we live our whole lives scared to death?" she asked. She pounded a fist on the table, making the ceramic fruit bowl shake. An apple rolled onto the floor. "I have to do something. I have to find Livvy. I have to talk to her . . . convince her to come back."

"Maybe she *was* back," Ana-Li said softly. "Maybe she was that bat. Maybe she came back to warn you."

"To warn me of what?"

"To stay away from her. To leave her alone."

Destiny grabbed her friend's arm. "That's crazy, Ana-Li. She's my sister. My twin sister. We belong together. She must know that. Even the way she is now . . . she must know that I'll do anything to bring her back to us."

"I have to go," Ana-Li said, moving quickly to the front door. "I have to get out of here. I mean, out of Dark Springs. It's too terrifying here. Bats and vampires and people dying. I'm so glad I'm going to New Haven in a few weeks."

She turned at the door. Destiny could see tears in her eyes. "I'm sorry, Dee," she said in a voice trembling with emotion. "I didn't mean to sound so cold. I know you've lost your sister. I didn't mean to sound selfish. I just . . . I . . ."

She spun away and disappeared out the door.

Ari stepped over to Destiny and wrapped her in a hug. "That was so horrible," he said softly. "That bat . . . when it attacked you, I—"

She silenced him with a kiss. The kiss lasted a long time. She wrapped her hands around his neck and held onto him, and they pressed together tightly as they kissed.

"You . . . you're going away, too," she whispered, finally pulling her lips away. She pressed her cheek against his. "You're going away too."

"Not until August. We have five weeks," he said.

She sighed. They kissed again. She shut her eyes and tried not to think about Ari leaving.

"About tonight," he said, holding her in his arms. "I know we have dinners with our parents tonight. But we can go out later. It's graduation, Dee. Let's go to that dance club that just opened. You know, Rip. Let's go there tonight, and pretend everything is okay . . . just for one night."

His eyes burned into hers. "Okay? Please say yes."

"Yes," Destiny agreed in a whisper.

"Hey, all right!" Ari pumped his fists in the air in victory.

Destiny started to kiss him again, but they were interrupted by a shout from upstairs.

Mikey, at the top of the stairs.

"Dee—hurry! Livvy's back! She's back! Hurry!"

chapter eleven

RIP

DESTINY RAN UP THE STAIRS, PULLING HERSELF UP
two steps at a time. At the top, Mikey grabbed her hand and
pulled her to his room.

Destiny blinked in the darkness. Mikey kept the blinds
closed, curtains pulled, and the lights off. "Where is she?"
Destiny cried. "I can't see anything."

She fumbled for the light switch and clicked on the ceiling light.

"No—don't!" Mikey grabbed her hand and pulled it
away from the light switch. "Turn it off. Turn it off."

Destiny obediently shut off the light.

"I was only pretending," Mikey said.

"You mean—?"

"I was pretending Livvy was back. That's all."

Destiny let out a long sigh. "Not again, Mikey." She

hugged him tightly. "Not again. You have to stop this. Do you understand?"

Mikey didn't reply.

Rip was a tall, barnlike building on the edge of North Town, the old section of Dark Springs. The club had previously been called Trixx, and before that Wild Weasel. Every year a new owner painted the outside a different color and put up new signs. But the inside was always pretty much the same.

As Destiny followed Ari inside, she saw a tall DJ wearing a white cowboy hat hunched over two turntables on a small stage in the center of the room. Red and blue neon lightning bolts flashed over the high ceiling, the light flickered off the dancers, dozens of them jammed together on the dance floor, moving to the throbbing rhythm, the music so loud the concrete floor vibrated.

A long, mirrored bar curved the length of the back wall. Low couches and fat armchairs formed a lounge on one side. Destiny looked up and saw people gazing down onto the dance floor from the narrow balcony that circled the room.

"I'll get us some beers," Ari said, leading her through the crowd. He opened his wallet and flashed a driver's license. "I have great fake I.D. A guy sold me this for fifty dollars, and it always works."

Eyes on the dancers, she followed him to the bar. Half the graduating class from Dark Springs High is here tonight, Destiny realized. She waved to some girls she knew. She spotted Ana-Li sitting in a big armchair in the lounge, leaning forward to talk to two guys Destiny had never seen before.

In a corner by the lounge, a girl in a sparkly red mini-dress was lip-locked with a guy in black jeans and a muscle shirt. He had a tattoo of a motorcycle on his bicep. As they kissed, he ran his big hands through her blond hair.

Blond hair . . .

No, Destiny thought. Not tonight. I'm not going to think about Livvy tonight.

But she stared at the girl kissing the big, tattooed guy so passionately, and she couldn't help but picture her sister there.

"Here you go." Ari bumped her shoulder. She turned and reached for the beer bottle in his hand. "The guy carded me," Ari said, grinning. "The Delaware driver's license always works. Want me to get you one?"

She frowned at him. "Ari, you don't even *like* beer that much. What's the big deal?"

He shrugged. "Come on. We're at a club, right? We gotta drink beer. Besides, I've got a lot of time to make up for. All those years, sitting in my room at the computer, going to dorky UFO websites or watching *Star Trek* reruns. I didn't know what I was missing!"

Ari has changed a lot, Destiny thought. I guess all the terrible things that have happened snapped him out of his fantasy world.

Ari started to raise the beer bottle to his mouth—and Fletch Green grabbed it out of his hand. "Thanks, dawg." Fletch emptied the bottle in less than five seconds and handed it back to Ari, a big smile on his face.

Ari stared at the empty beer bottle.

"Sorry you guys missed my party last night," Fletch said, sliding an arm around Destiny. "Hey, Dee, you look hot tonight."

Destiny wore a short, pleated black skirt, a tight, white midriff top, and her favorite red strappy sandals.

"So do you, Fletch," Destiny shot back. He was wearing baggy cargo pants and a black T-shirt with a martini glass on the front.

"It was a great party," Fletch said. "The cops came out three times. We have totally obnoxious neighbors. They call the cops if I sneeze too loud. But it was awesome. Gil Marx threw up in the fishpond. That was kinda gross. But no one else got too sick."

He took Destiny's beer from her hand and finished that one too. He handed the bottle to Ari. "Thanks again, dawg. You know, you're too young to drink." He gave the back of Destiny's hair a playful tug. Then he spun away and shambled off.

"Is he here with someone?" Ari asked, watching Fletch push his way through the dance floor.

Destiny shrugged. "Beats me. I heard he's been drinking a lot. I mean, a *lot*." She sighed. "The poor guy. He and Ross were like this." She held two fingers together. "I think he's a little lost without him."

"Hey, I thought we weren't going to talk about that tonight," Ari snapped. He clinked the empty bottles together. "I'll get another round."

"Not now." Destiny grabbed his arm. "Let's dance, okay?"

But he was already pushing his way to the bar.

What's he trying to prove? Destiny wondered. I thought we came here to dance.

Ari returned a few minutes later with two more beers. He downed his quickly and went back for another.

Destiny sipped hers slowly. She talked with three girls from her class, shouting over the throbbing dance music. They talked about how boring the graduation speaker was, their summer jobs, and what they planned to do in the fall.

Destiny could see the girls were a little uncomfortable. They were trying hard not to mention Livvy. Finally, one of them said, "Have you heard from your sister?"

"No," Destiny replied. "We don't know where she and Ross went."

She saw Ari at the bar, talking to a short, red-haired girl, tossing back another beer. Was he flirting with her?

Destiny made her way through the crowd and grabbed him by the elbow. "Are we going to dance or what?" She pulled him onto the dance floor.

They danced for a while under the flashing lightning bolts. Destiny shut her eyes and tried to lose herself to the music, the soaring voices, the insistent beat.

When she opened her eyes she saw Ana-Li nearby, dancing with one of the guys from the lounge. Ana-Li looked great in low-riding, black denims and a green tube top that showed a lot of skin. They waved to each other. Ana-Li pointed to Ari. They both laughed.

Yes, he was a terrible dancer. He had no sense of rhythm at all. Thrashing his arms around, bending his knees, Destiny thought he looked like a puppet that had lost his strings.

Destiny put her hands on Ari's shoulders and tried to guide him. He gave her a lopsided smile. His eyes were cloudy. How many beers had he drunk?

They danced for a long while. Destiny loved the feel of the floor vibrating beneath her, the lights pulsing, the constant beat of the dance music shutting out all other sound.

Ari had a good idea, she decided. I'm actually enjoying myself.

Then she saw the blond again, the one who reminded her so much of Livvy. She was dancing with her back to Destiny, swaying to the music with her arms above her head, her blond hair swinging from side to side.

With a sigh, Destiny stopped dancing. She stumbled into Ari. Her eyes were locked on the blond in the red mini-dress.

The kind of sexy outfit Livvy would wear. Her hair swinging like Livvy's.

"I . . . can't do this," she told Ari, holding onto him with both hands.

She pulled him off the dance floor. They found a small, round table near the bar and sat down. "What happened?" Ari asked, holding her hand.

"I can't do this," Destiny repeated. "I can't be here dancing and pretending."

"Hey, we came here to have fun, right?" Ari said, rolling his eyes. "Just for once, can't we forget about what's happening?"

"I tried," Destiny said. She found a tissue in her bag and wiped the sweat off her forehead. "But Livvy is out there somewhere." She pointed to the door. "Out in the night. My sister alone in the night. How can I—"

"It's not your fault," Ari shouted. "She made a stupid choice. She made a totally *selfish* choice. She didn't think about you, Dee. Or your father. Or your brother. She only thought about herself. So why are you thinking about *her* all the time? Why can't you lighten up for just one night?"

"You don't understand—" Destiny started. "Knowing that she's out there somewhere, prowling around, searching for God-knows-what, it's . . . it's worse than if she were dead."

Ari jumped up, a scowl on his face. "Give me a break," he muttered. "Enough already." He turned and stormed away, disappearing into the crowd on the dance floor.

"Ari, no—wait!" Destiny jumped to her feet and started after him. She bumped into a guy on the dance floor, then pushed past another couple. The flashing lights started to hurt her eyes, made her blink. The steady, pulsating beats began to pound in her ears.

"Ari——?"

Where was he?

I tried. I really tried, Destiny thought. I understand why he lost it. He's been so patient. He wants to have a little fun before he goes off to college. And I haven't been able to shake off this sadness.

She edged her way to the other side of the dance floor. No sign of Ari. Ana-Li stood with a Coke in one hand, talking to Fletch Green and two other guys from their class.

Destiny rushed up to her. "Have you seen Ari?"

Ana-Li laughed. "You lost him?"

"Kinda." Destiny didn't feel like telling her what happened.

"Lookin' hot, Dee," Jerry Freed, one of the three guys, said, grinning at her. He flashed her a thumbs-up.

Ana-Li pointed to the dance floor with her Coke can. "Isn't that Ari over there? Who's he dancing with?"

Destiny spun around. Squinting into the blinking lights, she saw Ari dancing with his hands on the bare waist of another girl . . . the red-haired girl he'd been flirting with at the bar. He pulled her close, and they danced cheek-to-cheek even though the music pounded even faster.

"I don't believe it," Destiny groaned.

"Did you two break up or something?" Ana-Li asked.

"Looks like it," Destiny said. She started toward Ari and his new dancing partner.

What is his problem? Is he just trying to hurt me?

He's been totally understanding the whole time, Destiny thought. Was it all an act?

She grabbed his arm. "Ari?"

He took his hands off the girl's waist, blinking at Destiny. "Oh. Hi." As if he didn't recognize her.

The red-haired girl frowned at Destiny and continued to move to the music.

"Ari, what's up with this?" Destiny couldn't keep her voice from trembling. "I mean—"

Ari shrugged.

"I mean, what's going on?"

"Just dancing."

She realized her hands were balled into tight fists. Working the turntables, the DJ went into a scratching fit, then changed the rhythm, drum machine pounding in her ears.

"Ari, I thought you and I—"

"Give me a break," Ari said.

The second time he said that tonight, Destiny told herself.

Well, okay. I'm not the kind of person who makes a big scene or screams or carries on in front of people. I can't do that.

So . . . I'll give him a break.

"Good night, Ari," she said through gritted teeth.

She spun away and ran along the side of the dance floor, ran without looking back, out the front door, bursting through a couple just arriving. Out into the cool night air, to the edge of the gravel parking lot, where she grabbed onto a wooden fence pole, held onto it, taking breath after breath.

Okay, okay. I'll give him a break, she thought.

Was she angry or hurt, or both?

Have fun, Ari. Have fun without me.

See if I care.

Destiny had no way of knowing that she would never see Ari again.

part four

chapter twelve

LIVVY'S
NEW LOVE

LIVVY STOOD AT THE END OF THE BAR, TILTING A bottle of Rolling Rock to her mouth. The bartender was a fat, old guy; not interesting. Despite the cold beer, Livvy's stomach growled, and the hunger gnawed at her.

She turned and gazed around the dance floor, searching for Monica and Suzie. Squinting into the darting red and blue lights, she spotted them both. Whoa. Who was Suzie dancing with? Ari Stark?

Uh-oh. Looks like Destiny left her boyfriend behind.

Bad mistake, Dee. Look at the stupid grin on Ari's face. He thinks he's gotten lucky tonight.

Monica stood at the edge of the dance floor, her pale arms around a big guy who looked like he could play middle linebacker. She nestled her head against his shoulder and led him toward the lounge.

Way to go, Monica.

Feeling the powerful hunger again, Livvy brushed back her blond hair, straightened her tube top, and gazed down the bar. A dark-haired guy a few stools down seemed to be staring at her.

Livvy flashed him a smile. He had a beer glass in one hand. He raised it as if toasting her.

Livvy didn't hesitate. She strode over to him, a smile on her face. "I'm Livvy," she said. "How ya doin'?"

"Patrick," he replied. He had dimples in his cheeks when he smiled. He was probably a college guy—in his early twenties—cute.

Livvy clicked her bottle against his glass. "What's up, Patrick?"

He shrugged. "Just chillin'. You know."

He had short, wavy brown hair, dark, serious eyes with heavy, brown eyebrows, and a penetrating stare. Livvy felt that he was staring right through her.

Did he like what he saw?

Livvy did. If the good-looking guys have the tastiest blood, I'm in heaven tonight.

Patrick was tall and athletic-looking. He wore black cargo pants and a dark brown leather vest over a soft gray long-sleeved shirt. An interesting look.

He had a silver ring in one ear. And Livvy glimpsed a tattoo of a spider on the back of his hand when he raised his beer glass.

"Like this club?" Livvy asked, squeezing beside him.

Wouldn't you rather go out for a drink, Patrick?

Out to the woods maybe?

"Yeah, it's okay," he said. "I don't like the five-dollar beers. But it's a pretty nice place to hang."

Livvy flashed him her sexiest smile. "I think it just got nicer," she said. Not too subtle, but she felt too hungry to be subtle.

He has a nice long neck, she thought. Easy to get to the vein.

Was she staring at his throat? She quickly raised her eyes to his. "I wouldn't mind dancing," she said. "If someone wanted to ask me."

He was a good dancer, she discovered. He moved easily, gracefully, and never took his eyes off her. When he smiled, those dimples came out, and despite her hunger, Livvy could feel herself melting.

Is this my night or what?

Suzie came into view across the crowded dance floor. Over Ari's shoulder, she flashed Livvy a thumbs-up.

After a while, Patrick took Livvy's hand and led her off the dance floor. She squeezed his hand and leaned against him. Even though they'd been dancing hard, he wasn't sweating. He bought two more Rolling Rocks at the bar and handed one to her.

"I haven't seen you here before," he said.

Livvy grinned. "You're seeing me now." She took a sip of beer. "What do you do, Patrick?"

He snickered. "As little as possible. How about you?"

"I'm in school," she lied. She put a hand on his shoulder. "It's kinda hot in here. And noisy. Want to take a walk or something?"

Say yes, Patrick—or I might attack you right here.

"Yeah, sure," he said, finishing his beer. "But I've gotta tell some guys I came with, okay?"

Livvy nodded. *Tell them you're going out for a quick bite, Patrick.* She felt her heart start to race. Her skin tingled.

I'm finally going to feed.

"Meet you outside," she said. "I'm going to smoke."

She watched him make his way through the dance floor. He had a quick, confident stride. He's hot, she thought. Too hot to die. Maybe I'll bring him along slowly. Then give him a chance to join me, to become an immortal. To live forever with me.

She started toward the exit.

Then what do I do with Ross?

Good question.

I still care for Ross. He was so brave to come with me to the other side. He'd be lost without me . . .

Ross is so sweet. But maybe sweet isn't what I need right now. I need thrills. I need action. I need to live this new life to the fullest.

I need . . . Patrick.

As Livvy passed the lounge, she glimpsed Monica in a dark corner, on a low couch, lip-locked with the guy she'd been dancing with. Monica was pressed against him, holding his head as she kissed him, moving her hands through the guy's hair.

He's toast, Livvy thought.

She stepped out into the night. The air felt cool on her hot skin. Clouds covered the moon. A car squealed out of the parking lot, music blaring.

Livvy stepped to the side of the club, leaned against the stucco wall, and pulled a pack of Camel Reds from her bag. She slid a cigarette between her lips. And felt a soft tap on her shoulder.

Patrick?

She spun around—and let out a startled gasp. "*You?* What are *you* doing here? *Get away!*"

chapter thirteen

A SURPRISE
REUNION

THE CIGARETTE FELL FROM HER MOUTH. LIVVY stared at her sister, at her black skirt and white top, her blond hair pulled straight back so neatly, her plastic bracelets on one wrist, everything so neat and perfect.

Except what was that expression on Destiny's face? Eyes so wide and chin quivering. Destiny stared at Livvy as if she'd never seen her before.

And was that fear in her eyes?

"Destiny, go away," Livvy repeated. "I don't want to see you."

"I'm your sister." Destiny's voice trembled. "Why are you saying that?"

Livvy stared at her. "I'm busy right now. I'm waiting for someone. Take a walk, Dee. I mean it."

Destiny swallowed. She didn't move. "You look so different. You cut your hair. You've lost weight, haven't you. And those dark rings around your eyes—"

"Hey, no beauty tips, okay," Livvy snarled. "I don't read *Cosmo Girl* anymore."

"You're so pale, Livvy," Destiny continued. "You look as if you haven't slept in weeks. Listen to me—"

"No, you listen to me, Dee," Livvy said through clenched teeth. "Read my lips: *Go away*." She glanced over Destiny's shoulder. Where was Patrick?

"Was that you this afternoon?" Destiny asked, crossing her arms in front of her. "The bat?"

"Excuse me?" Livvy pulled another cigarette from the pack. Her hand shook as she slid it between her lips. "What bat? I don't know what the hell you're talking about."

"It wasn't you?"

"No way. Were you dreaming or something?"

I don't know why I did that, Livvy thought, remembering the afternoon. I'll never do it again.

"I thought I saw you in the club," Destiny said, motioning to the entrance with her head. "You didn't see me, did you? I was with Ari. But I think he left. We had a fight. I feel terrible. He's so sweet."

"Tell someone who cares," Livvy said. She yawned.

Destiny startled her by grabbing her arm. "Come home, Liv. Come home with me right now."

Livvy rolled her eyes. "Yeah, sure. Good idea." She tugged her arm free.

"No, really," Destiny insisted. "Dad will find a cure. I know he will. He's working so hard, Liv. He'll find a cure for you, and you can be normal again. You know. Back home."

Livvy let out an angry cry. "You never could stand to see me have fun!" she shouted. "Get a clue, Dee. I don't want to go back to that boring life."

"Yes, you do," Destiny replied, tears in her eyes. "You don't mean what you're saying. You can't like what you're doing. The way you're living. You *can't*." A sob escaped her throat.

Livvy took a deep breath. Her hands were clenched into tight fists at her sides. "Don't you see? I've made my choice. I'm going to live forever. That's my choice. You want to stay home and see your boring friends and that boring geek Ari, and go to school like a nice girl and be a nice, boring person for the rest of your life. And I've made a different choice. That's all. No big deal, right?"

"But, Liv—"

"I'm going to live forever. That's my choice. So get out of my face, Dee. Go away and don't come back."

"I . . . don't believe you." Destiny let the tears roll down her cheeks. "You're my sister. My *twin* sister. And the two of us belong together. We—"

"We belong together? Okay!" Livvy cried. She let her fangs slide down over her lips. "You want to stay together forever? Fine. You stay with *me*."

She grabbed Destiny around the waist and started to

drag her across the parking lot toward the woods.

"Hey—let go!" Destiny screamed, unable to hide her panic. "What are you doing?"

"We'll be together," Livvy growled, saliva running down her fangs. "You and me. Together."

Destiny grabbed Livvy's arms and tried to pull them off her. But Livvy held onto her tightly and dragged her over the gravel toward the tall trees.

"You and me," Livvy rasped. "Just the way you want it, Dee."

"Let go! Let go!" Destiny pleaded.

Livvy pressed her mouth against the back of Destiny's neck. "You and me—forever," she whispered.

chapter fourteen

THE TASTE
OF NIGHT

LIVVY HELD ON TIGHT AS DESTINY SQUIRMED AND struggled to free herself. Finally, she gave Dee's hair a hard tug—and let her go.

Destiny staggered forward several steps. Then she spun around to face her sister. "Were you . . . were you . . ." She struggled to catch her breath. "What were you doing? Were you just trying to scare me?"

Livvy grinned at her. She made loud sucking noises with her fangs. "Want to stay and find out?"

Trembling, Destiny studied her for a long moment. Then she turned and ran across the parking lot.

Livvy watched her sister run away. Her heart was pounding in her chest. She suddenly felt dizzy.

I'm so confused. My feelings are all mixed up.

I always loved Destiny. Do I really hate her now?

Is it because she's trying to ruin my new life?

I made my choice. Why can't she leave me alone?

Livvy turned and saw Patrick watching her from the club exit. She slid her fangs back into her gums. Then she straightened her hair and forced a sexy smile to her face.

"There you are," he called, taking those long strides toward her. "I thought maybe you split or something."

"No way." She took his arm. "It's nice out, huh?"

He nodded. She liked his serious, dark eyes, the way they seemed to lock on her as if holding her captive.

The clouds floated away from the moon, and pale light washed over them. "I like the moonlight," he said, glancing up at the sky.

"How old are you?" she asked, leaning against him, guiding him to the trees.

"Old enough," he said. "How old did you think I was?"

"I don't know. Inside the club, you looked sixteen. But now you look older." She let her hand slide down his arm and gripped his hand. "I'm going to be eighteen soon."

"Are you in college?" he asked. Their shoes crunched over the gravel. He didn't wait for her to answer. He turned and kissed her. He held her chin in his hand and kissed her long and deep.

Yes, she thought. And as she kissed him, a strange phrase played through her mind . . .

The taste of night.

The taste of night.

Where did it come from? She didn't know. But she knew she was enjoying it tonight—the taste of night. The taste of the cool, fresh air and the moonlight, the taste of his lips, the taste of an exciting, new adventure. And in a few moments . . . the taste of blood.

It was all part of the taste of night.

I'm totally into him, she thought. I mean I'm really attracted to him. He's so good looking and mysterious and sexy.

We just met, but I already have strong feelings for him, she realized.

Almost as strong as my thirst . . .

He pulled his face away. They were both breathing hard. He still had his hand on her chin. "Where are you leading me?" he asked.

She grinned. "Astray?"

He laughed. A big laugh that seemed to come from deep inside him.

"I thought we'd take a walk in the woods," Livvy said. "Such a nice night. We can talk. It's so peaceful out here."

"You're an outdoors-type person? You like to camp?"

"Not really," she replied. "But I like to do *other* things in the woods." She pulled him into the trees. The moonlight seemed to follow them. She pulled him farther. She needed darkness.

"Hey, where are we going? I can't see a thing," he said, tugging her to a stop.

"That's the idea," she whispered. She grabbed the sides

of his head and pulled his face to hers. They kissed again, moving their tongues together.

I'm so hungry, she thought.

I can't wait another second.

I need to drink. He's driving me crazy.

She pulled her lips from his and nuzzled his ear with her mouth. "Now, Patrick, I'm going to give you a kiss to remember," she whispered. "But here's the sad part. After I give it to you, I'm going to cloud your mind so you won't remember it."

"Huh? I don't understand." He held her by the waist and stared into her eyes. "What are you saying?"

So hungry . . . so hungry . . . Oh, damn—I'm so hungry . . .

Livvy lowered her fangs and dug them into his throat. Deep, deep into the soft flesh.

And then she pulled away—and opened her mouth in a scream of horror.

chapter fifteen

"I'M NOT
JUST A VAMPIRE"

LIVVY STAGGERED BACK, STUMBLING OVER AN upraised tree root and landing hard against the fat trunk of a maple tree. Patrick didn't move. He stood still as a statue, a shadow against shadows.

"You . . . you're a vampire too," she whispered finally. She struggled to catch her breath. Her body still tingled from the excitement of nearly finding blood.

But Patrick's blood wouldn't nourish her.

He stepped closer, and she could see the smile on his face. "I'm sorry," he said. "I wanted to see how far you'd go."

Her surprise quickly turned to anger. "You were just playing a game? Having a little joke at my expense?"

He took her hand. "No. It wasn't just a joke. I really like you."

"What were you doing in the club?" Livvy asked.

"Same as you. Looking to hook up."

"But I wasn't looking to hook up with a vampire. I'm so hungry," Livvy moaned. "You've wasted my time."

He laughed. "Hey, don't hurt my feelings. I said I really like you."

"But I don't need a vampire. I need—" Livvy started.

He put a finger over her lips. "I'm not just a vampire, Livvy. Things are going to change now that I'm here."

"Excuse me?" She let go of his hand. "What are you talking about?"

"I'm going to take care of everyone. Make it a lot more exciting for all of us."

Moonlight filtered through the trees, and Livvy could see his smile and his eyes, crazy eyes, intense and unblinking. He seemed to be aiming all his power at her.

She turned away.

"Where do you live?" she asked.

"Same building as you," he replied

She kept her eyes away from his. "How do you know where I live? You've seen me before?"

"Truth? I've had my eye on you."

"You've been watching me? Why?" she asked.

He didn't answer. He pulled her close, lowered his face to hers, and kissed her. Kissed her hard, so hard she could feel his teeth pressing against her lips . . . so hard it hurt.

When the kiss ended, her lips throbbed with pain.

Heart pounding, she pressed her forehead against the front of his shirt.

Livvy realized she was trembling. I'm hot for him—and I'm afraid of him—at the same time.

Patrick took her by the shoulders and moved her away. "It's getting late. I'm thirsty too."

"But I want to know more about you," Livvy said. She flashed him a grin. "You can't just take a girl into the woods and leave her there."

Once again, he brought his face to hers. And he whispered in her ear. "Later."

He whirled away from her—and transformed quickly into a slender red fox. Squinting into the patch of silvery moonlight, Livvy watched the fox scamper away through the thick underbrush.

Yes, later, she thought.

Catch you later, Patrick. I think you and I are going to be seeing a lot of each other.

chapter sixteen

DESTINY
FLIES

DESTINY SEARCHED FOR ARI IN THE CLUB BUT couldn't find him. She wanted to apologize. He was only *dancing* with that red-haired girl, after all. She shouldn't have embarrassed him by acting so jealous.

This night is a disaster, she thought. No way is it a celebration.

She ended up walking home by herself. The night air felt cool against her hot skin. Crickets chirped. Fireflies danced in front of her, seeming to light her path. The moon appeared and disappeared behind high, gray clouds.

She walked through tall grass along the side of the road. Her shoes became wet from the dew. Cars rolled past without slowing.

She found herself thinking about Ross. She wondered

how he was. She couldn't picture Ross as a vampire. He was so good looking and athletic and . . . healthy.

Destiny had a crush on Ross for years, and Livvy knew it. But Livvy went after Ross anyway. And she took him away.

Forever.

The tiny lights of fireflies sparkled in Destiny's eyes, making the world appear unreal. The lights darted and danced around her.

Before she knew it, she arrived at Drake Park, three blocks from her house. As she crossed the street and stepped into the park, she could hear the trickle of water from the narrow creek and the rustle of the trees shaking in the warm breeze.

She followed the dirt path that curved toward her house. A creature scampered over her feet, startling her. A field mouse? A chipmunk?

She thought about Mikey. What did he do tonight? The poor kid. I hope he didn't spend the whole night shut up in his dark cave of a room.

Destiny told herself she should spend more time with Mikey. But it wasn't easy. Tomorrow morning she was starting her summer job at the Four Corners Diner. A waitress behind the lunch counter. Not a very challenging job. But at least the restaurant was across from the Community College campus. Maybe she'd meet some new people . . .

The moon disappeared behind a blanket of clouds. The fireflies had vanished. Destiny felt a chill as the darkness washed over her.

She kicked a stone in the path. The creek trickled behind her now. She knew she was almost home.

And then a figure stepped out from a thick clump of pine trees. A girl. She seemed to float silently onto the path.

"Hello—?" Destiny called in a whisper.

The girl didn't answer. She moved toward Destiny quickly. Startled, Destiny began to move out of the way, but she wasn't quick enough.

"Hey—" Destiny let out a cry—and then recognized her sister. "Livvy? What are you doing here?"

Livvy stared at her for a long moment, her expression intense, eyes locked on Destiny's.

Why did Livvy follow me? To apologize?

Did she change her mind about coming home?

And then to Destiny's shock, Livvy raised both arms and wrapped her in a tight hug.

The two sisters stood there on the dark path, hugging each other, faces pressed together, tears rolling down their cheeks, tears running together as they sobbed and held each other.

Finally, they backed away from each other. They both wiped away tears with their hands.

"Livvy, I'm so happy," Destiny said in a trembling whisper. "Why did you follow me? Did you change your mind?"

"Yes," Livvy replied. "Yes, I changed my mind. I . . . I'm so lonely, Dee. I need to come home. I need to be with my family again."

"Dad and Mikey . . . they'll be so glad to see you," Destiny said.

And then the two sisters were hugging again, hugging and crying.

Destiny finally released her sister. "Let's go home," she whispered. "It's late, but Dad will still be awake. He doesn't sleep much—ever since . . ." Her voice trailed off.

Livvy clung to her sister. She didn't reply.

"I'm so glad," Destiny said. "I mean, I'm so happy, Liv. I mean . . . I can't really say what I mean."

Livvy's arms remained clamped tightly around Destiny. Her head was turned so that Destiny couldn't see her face.

"Please let go," Destiny whispered. "I . . . can't breathe."

Livvy didn't move.

"Let go," Destiny repeated. "Come on. Let's go home, okay?"

Livvy didn't reply. Her arms remained clamped around Destiny's waist.

"Livvy—let go!" Destiny cried. "What's wrong? What are you doing? Let go of me. Let go!"

Destiny tried to pull free. And as she squirmed and twisted, she saw Livvy's body begin to transform.

"Livvy—stop! What are you doing? Let go of me—please!"

And now, scratchy brown feathers scraped Destiny's face. She heard a warble from deep inside Livvy's body. And she realized that powerful claws, hard as bone, had replaced her sister's arms.

Livvy had transformed into an enormous, throbbing bird, at least seven feet tall. A giant hawk! And Destiny was pressed tightly against the prickly feathers around its belly, held by the huge, powerful claws clamped around her waist.

"Livvy—NO!"

The bird raised its head, flapped its massive wings, sending a burst of air over Destiny. It dragged Destiny along the grass for a while before it lifted high enough into the air. And then, flapping its wings so slowly, so easily, it floated up into the dark sky, carrying Destiny in its claws like a prize . . . like dinner.

Destiny let out scream after scream as she floated over the treetops of the park, then the houses of her neighborhood.

Is she planning to drop me?

The houses looked like dollhouses now. The car headlights down below looked as tiny as the firefly light that had followed her as she walked.

"Livvy—please!"

She could feel the pattering heartbeat of the huge bird. The oily feathers grazed her cheeks.

And then they were soaring down, swooping with the wind. The onrushing wind blowing so hard in her face, Destiny struggled to breathe.

A hard bounce. The claws let go. Destiny landed on her back. Felt the air knocked out of her. Lay there on hard ground, gasping.

Where are we?

Livvy loomed over her, human once again. Livvy's hair fell over her face, but Destiny could see her eyes. Wild eyes, bulging with anger . . . with hate?

"Where are we? Where have you taken me?" Destiny cried. She raised herself on two arms and gazed around, blinking in the darkness.

Nothing to see. No trees here. No houses. Flat ground, a black strip against the blacker sky, stretching on forever.

"Where are we?"

"It doesn't matter, Dee." Livvy spoke in a cold whisper. "It really doesn't matter."

"Why? What do you mean?"

Livvy narrowed her eyes at Destiny, and her face hardened to stone. "Because you're never leaving."

"I don't understand, Livvy. What—?"

Livvy's fangs slid quickly from her gums, making a loud *pok* sound. She opened her mouth wide, tongue playing over her teeth, drool running over her chin. Then she sank her fangs deep into Destiny's throat.

chapter seventeen

TROUBLE AT
ARI'S HOUSE

DESTINY FELT SWEAT RUN DOWN HER FOREHEAD. Her nightshirt clung wetly to her back.

She blinked, reached a hand to her throat, and smoothed two fingers across it.

No wound.

She blinked some more, realizing she was gazing into bright sunlight. From the bedroom window.

She jerked herself upright, breathing hard. A dream? Yes.

It had been a dream—all of it. I didn't walk home last night, she remembered. Fletch Green gave me a ride.

But the feeling of walking home through the park . . . the sparkling fireflies . . . her sister stepping out of the darkness . . . transforming into the gigantic hawk . . . All so real.

So real she thought she could still feel those bonelike

claws wrapped tightly around her waist. She could still feel the suffocating rush of wind as the giant bird carried her into the sky.

Could still feel Livvy's fangs . . .

Does my twin sister really have fangs?

A soft cry escaped Destiny's throat. Yes, it was a dream. But the rest of my life is real . . .

. . . and it's a nightmare.

"Dee! Dee!" She heard Mikey calling from downstairs. She jumped out of bed, gazing at the clock radio on her bedtable.

Oh, no. Late. I have to give Mikey breakfast and get him off to day camp. She brushed her teeth, pushed back her hair with her hands, and went running down to the kitchen in her nightshirt.

"Where's Dad?" she asked Mikey.

He was dressed in denim shorts that came down past his knees and a blue-and-red Camp Redhawk T-shirt about five sizes too big for him. He gripped a stuffed lion in one hand. He'd had it since he was a baby. These days it looked more like a washcloth than a lion.

He shrugged. "Work. He woke me up. Then he left. I'm hungry. And so is Lester." He waved Lester the Lion in Destiny's face.

She popped two frozen waffles into the toaster. "We're a little late. You'll have to eat your waffles fast."

"Take the crust off," he said, sitting down at the table, plopping Lester in front of him.

Destiny turned to him. "Crust on waffles?"

"Yeah. Take off the crust."

He had become the fussiest eater. He suddenly had rules for everything. And he found something wrong with everything put in front of him. A few nights ago, he had even refused to eat the french fries at Burger King because they were "too curled up."

She poured him a glass of orange juice and handed it to him. "No pulp," she said before he could ask.

He tasted it gingerly, a tiny sip. "Too cold."

"What are you doing at day camp today?" she asked, brushing back his thick mop of hair with one hand.

"I'm not going to day camp," Mikey replied. He pounded Lester on the tabletop for emphasis.

"You have to go," Destiny said, lifting the waffles from the toaster. "Ow. Hot. There's no one here to take care of you."

"You can take care of me," he said.

"No, I can't, Mikey. You know that I'm starting my summer job today, remember?"

"Well, I can't go to camp. Hey—you forgot to cut off the crusts. And I don't want butter. I want syrup."

Destiny took the plate back and carefully pulled the edges off the waffles. "And why can't you go to camp?"

"Because they're showing a movie at the theater." He took another swallow of orange juice.

"You like movies," Destiny said, handing the plate back to him. "So what's the problem?"

"It . . . it's cold and creepy in the theater," he replied. "There might be vampires in there."

Destiny stopped in front of the diner and checked her hair and lipstick in her reflection in the front window. The name FOUR CORNERS DINER was painted in fancy gold script across the wide window.

Destiny chuckled. It seemed an odd name for the little restaurant since it was located in the middle of the block. Surrounding it on both sides were small, two-story brick and shingle buildings that contained clothing stores, a bank, a CD store—shops that catered to Community College students.

She turned and glanced at the campus. Four square, granite buildings around a narrow rectangle of patchy grass and trees. Not the most beautiful campus in the world.

Destiny let out a sigh. I made the right decision, she told herself. I couldn't go away to college and leave Dad and Mikey now. I'll go to the Community College for a year or two. When things are more in control at home, I can transfer to a better school.

When things are more in control . . .

She turned and hurried into the diner. The smell of fried grease greeted her. Bright lights made the long lunch counter glow. A ceiling fan squeaked as it slowly turned.

Destiny counted three people seated at one end of the counter. Two guys about her age and an older woman. The four booths in back were empty. Mr. Georgio, the owner, stood behind the counter, setting down plates of hamburgers and french fries for the three customers.

"Mr. Georgio, sorry I'm a little late," Destiny said, glancing up at the round Coca-Cola clock above the coat rack in the corner. "I had trouble getting my brother off to day camp."

"Call me Mr. G., remember?" he said, setting plastic ketchup and mustard dispensers in front of the customers. He walked over to her, wiping sweat off his bald head with a paper napkin.

He was a thin, little man of forty or forty-five. The white apron he wore over black slacks and a white sport shirt hung nearly to the floor. He had big, brown eyes, a thick, brown mustache under his bulby nose, and a split between his front teeth that showed when he smiled.

"Late? No problem," he said. "We're not exactly packing them in today." He motioned with his head to the three customers.

"Summer is slow," he said, wiping a grease spot on the yellow counter. "Most of the students aren't here. There are only a few classes. My business is students. Breakfast and lunch. You'll have a nice, quiet time, Ms. Weller. You can read a book or something."

"Please, call me Dee. Remember?" Destiny said.

He smiled. "Okay, you're Dee and I'm G."

"Could we have more Cokes?" a guy at the end of the counter called, holding up his glass.

"Take care of them," Mr. G. told her, pulling off his apron. "And clean things up a bit, okay? I've got to go out."

He pointed to the kitchen window behind the counter. "You remember Nate? The fry cook? He's back there somewhere. Probably sneaking a smoke. He's a lazy goof-off. But if you have any questions, he'll help you out."

Destiny had worked some weekends at the diner, so she already knew her way around. She waved to Nate through the window, carried three glasses to the soda dispenser, and filled them with Coke.

The bell over the door clanged as two more customers came in. Destiny didn't recognize them at first because of the white sunlight pouring in through the front window. But as they settled into the first booth behind the counter, she saw that she knew them. Rachel Seeger and Bonnie Franz, two girls from her class.

Destiny picked up two menus and carried them over to the booth. Her two friends were talking heatedly, giggling and gesturing with their hands. But they stopped their conversation when they recognized Destiny.

Rachel's cheeks blushed bright pink. She had light blond hair and really fair skin and was an easy blusher, Destiny remembered. "Hey, Dee. What's up?" she asked.

"You waitressing here?" Bonnie asked.

Destiny laughed. "No. Just holding menus. It's like a hobby of mine."

The girls laughed.

"I have a summer job too," Bonnie said. "At the campus. I'm filing stuff in the administration office. Yawn yawn."

"Are you making any money?" Destiny asked.

Bonnie shook her head. "Eight dollars an hour. And my dad said he had to pull strings to get me the job. I mean, like hel-lo. I could make that at McDonald's, right?"

Destiny handed them the menus. "Know what you want?"

"Not really," Bonnie said.

"Are you working this summer?" Destiny asked Rachel.

She made a disgusted face. "I couldn't find anything. So I'm just hanging out this summer. You know. Partying. Getting ready for college. You're going away, right, Dee?"

"Uh . . . no." Destiny hesitated. She didn't want sympathy from her friends. "I decided to stay close to home and go here." She motioned out the window to the campus. "You know. It's kinda tough times at home . . ."

"Have you heard from your sister?" Rachel asked, blushing again. "I mean, she and Ross have been gone so long."

Destiny lowered her eyes to the yellow tabletop. "No. Haven't heard anything yet."

Rachel gripped the big, red menu with both hands. "Do the police still think they ran away together?"

Destiny saw Bonnie motioning for Rachel to shut up.

"The police . . . they don't know *what* to think," Destiny said honestly.

"Sorry," Bonnie muttered.

The two girls stared down at their menus. An awkward silence. The conversation had ended.

Destiny raised her pad to take their orders. Everyone treats me so differently now, she thought. I used to hang with Bonnie and Rachel and goof with them all the time. Once, a sales clerk at The Gap made us leave because we were laughing too loud in the dressing room.

But now, people feel sorry for me. They feel awkward. They don't know what to say.

"Could we have a check?" a woman called from the counter.

"I'll be right back," Destiny told the two girls. She hurried along the counter to take care of the woman's check.

As soon as she left, her two friends started chattering away again.

After work, Destiny decided to drive over to Ari's house. She'd been thinking about him all afternoon.

I'm going to apologize for last night, she decided. What happened at the club . . . it really was my fault.

Ari wanted to celebrate, to have some fun. And I was a total drag. I should have tried harder to forget my problems, to just go with the flow . . .

She pictured him dancing with that red-haired girl. Thinking about it gave her a heavy feeling in her stomach.

Ari is going off to school soon. And I'm going to miss him terribly. I have to be nicer to him.

Yes, I'm definitely going to apologize.

Thinking about last night, there was no way to shut out the memory of her meeting with Livvy. Turning onto Ari's block, sunlight burst over the windshield. And through the blinding white light, Destiny saw two blond girls standing on the front stoop of the corner house.

"Oh——!" she let out a cry.

The car moved under the shadow of trees. The two girls disappeared into the house.

Destiny frowned. Every time I see a girl with blond hair, I think it's my sister.

Livvy was so mean to me last night. Has she completely forgotten that we're sisters? It's only been a few weeks, and she has changed so much. She looked so pale and thin and . . . and worn out.

Livvy acted so cold and angry. I hardly recognized her.

Destiny saw the tall hedge in front of Ari's yard, the white-shingled house rising up behind it. She turned and pulled into the drive—and stopped.

"Hey—"

Two police squad cars blocked her way, red lights spinning on their roofs.

"Oh, no." Destiny's heart started to pound. She felt her throat tighten.

Ari's dad had a heart attack last summer. Has he had another one?

Hands trembling, she pulled the car to the curb in front of the neighbors' house. Then she went running up the driveway.

The front door was open. She burst inside. She heard voices in the front room. Someone crying.

"What's wrong?" she shouted breathlessly. "What's happened?"

chapter eighteen

WHO IS
THE NEXT VICTIM?

DESTINY RAN INTO THE LIVING ROOM. SHE SAW ARI'S mother hunched in the tall, green armchair by the fireplace. Her head was buried in a white handkerchief, and she was sobbing loudly, her shoulders heaving up and down.

Mr. Stark stood beside the chair, one hand on his wife's shoulder. He was very pale and, even from a distance, Destiny could see the tear tracks on his cheeks.

Two grim-faced, young police officers stood with their hands in their pockets, shaking their heads, speaking softly to Ari's parents. They spun around when Destiny entered the room.

"What is it? Where's Ari?" Destiny cried.

But even before anyone answered, she knew. She knew why they were crying. They had bad news about Ari. Maybe the *worst* news . . .

"No—!" Destiny screamed, pressing her hands against her face. "No. Please—"

No one had spoken. But she knew.

Mr. Stark came across the room to greet her, walking stiffly, as if it took all his effort. He was a tall, heavyset man, and now he was walking as if he weighed a thousand pounds.

He put his hands on Destiny's shoulders. "It's Ari," he whispered. "It's horrible, Dee. Ari . . . Ari . . ." He turned away from her.

"What . . . what happened to him?" Destiny stammered.

Mrs. Stark uttered a loud sob across the room.

One of the police officers studied Destiny.

"I'm Lieutenant Macy," he said, keeping his voice low. "Are you Destiny Weller?"

Destiny nodded. Her throat felt so tight, it was hard to breathe. "Yes. How did you know?"

"We've been trying to reach you all day," he said. "The phone at your house . . . it rang and rang."

"I started a new job today," Destiny said. "Is Ari—?"

Macy had bright blue eyes and he kept them trained on Destiny. "I'm sorry. He's . . . dead."

A cry escaped Destiny's throat. Her knees folded. She started to collapse to the floor, but Macy grabbed her gently by the arm and held her up.

She struggled to catch her breath. It felt as if her chest might burst open.

"Come sit down," Macy said softly. He led her to the green leather couch in front of the window.

Tears flowed down her cheeks. She fumbled in her bag for some tissues. "What happened?" she asked Macy. She gritted her teeth. She didn't really want to hear.

"We were hoping you could help us out with that," Macy said, leaning forward, bringing his face close to hers. "You were with Ari last night, right? You were at the dance club?"

Destiny nodded, dabbing at her tears. She glanced up to see Mr. Stark staring down at her, hunched behind Macy. She glimpsed the pain in his eyes and turned away.

"Well, a young couple found Ari at the edge of the parking lot there," Macy said. "It was about two A.M. Were you still with him then?"

Destiny stared at the officer. His voice sounded muffled, as if he were speaking underwater. Ari dead in the parking lot? Two in the morning? She struggled to make sense of it.

"No. I . . . left early," Destiny said finally.

Macy stared at her, waiting for more of an explanation.

"We had a fight," Destiny said. "Well, no. Not really a fight. An argument, I guess. And I . . . I left early."

"How early?" Macy asked.

"I left around midnight, I think. I got a ride home with a friend. I remember it was a little after twelve-thirty when I got home."

"And was Ari still at the club when you left?"

Destiny nodded. "I . . . think so. Yes. Yes, he was."

"You saw him there before you left?" Macy demanded.

Destiny nodded again, wiping at her tears. "He was

dancing. I saw him dancing . . . with another girl."

Across the room, Mrs. Stark uttered a loud sob. Mr. Stark hurried over to comfort her.

Destiny raised her eyes to Macy. "How . . . did Ari die?" she whispered.

Macy's blue eyes burned into hers. "Strangest thing. He had two puncture wounds in his neck. His blood was completely drained."

"Do you really think Livvy did it?" Ana-Li asked.

Destiny shook her head. "I don't know what to think."

They were sitting on the couch in Destiny's room above the garage, the room she had shared with her twin. The couch divided the long, low room in two. Destiny hadn't touched anything on Livvy's side. She'd left it exactly as Livvy had it.

When Livvy comes back, it will be ready for her.

That's what Destiny had thought. Until now.

"Livvy and I talked outside the club," Destiny told Ana-Li, folding her arms tightly in front of her. "We didn't really talk. We just screamed. I mean, Livvy did the screaming. She was awful to me. She . . . she's changed so much."

Ana-Li took a long sip from her Diet Coke can, her dark eyes on Destiny. "What did you fight about?"

"Nothing, really. I begged her to come home. She told me to leave her alone, to stay out of her life. That's all. But it was the way she said it. So cruel. As if she *hates* me."

Ana-Li squeezed Destiny's hand. Her hand was cold

from the soda can. "Livvy wasn't angry enough to murder Ari—was she? I mean, she's known Ari as long as you have. No way she'd murder him out of spite or something."

Destiny sighed. "I don't know. I don't know what to think anymore. I thought I knew her. I mean, she's my *twin* sister. But now . . . I don't know her at all."

"You can't believe she'd murder your boyfriend," Ana-Li said. "It had to be someone else, Dee. It's just too sick."

"Yeah. Sick," Destiny repeated. "That's the word. This whole thing is sick."

"What do the cops say?" Ana-Li asked.

"They've been back to question me three times. They interviewed the red-haired girl. She said she danced with Ari a couple of times, and then she didn't see him again. She thinks he went off with another girl, but she doesn't really know."

"That's a really busy parking lot," Ana-Li said. "Didn't anyone see anything strange going on?"

"So far, no one has called the police," Destiny replied.

"The police know there are vampires in Dark Springs," Ana-Li said, tapping a long, red nail fingernail on the Diet Coke can. "They help your father and his vampire hunters, right? So they must know—"

"They're trying to keep it quiet," Destiny interrupted. "The cops didn't reveal what really happened to Ari to the news people. They don't want to start a panic."

She let out a cry. "I just can't believe my own sister could do something so horrible. But she was there. And she told me how thirsty she was."

Ana-Li shuddered. She set down the soda can. "Dee, there's something I have to tell you."

Destiny blinked at her. "What?"

"I'm leaving for school early," Ana-Li said. "I can't stand it here anymore. I'm leaving on Saturday. It's just too frightening here. I have to get away."

Ana-Li didn't give Destiny time to reply. She hugged her, then turned and, with a sad wave, made her way down the stairs.

Destiny remained on the couch, feeling numb. Unable to stop the upsetting whirl of thoughts that troubled her mind.

Ari is dead.

Ana-Li is leaving.

My friends are all gone.

Will I be next?

Will I be the next victim?

part five

TWO WEEKS
LATER

chapter nineteen

"MAYBE HE'S JUST WHAT I NEED"

"TWO OVER EASY, SIDE OF TOAST," DESTINY SAID, poking her head through the window to the kitchen. Then she let out a startled gasp. "You're not Nate!"

The guy at the stove waved his metal spatula at her. "Hey, you're real sharp."

"Where's Nate?" Destiny asked, glancing around the tiny diner kitchen.

"Fired. Didn't Mr. G. tell you?"

"Guess he forgot. Who are you?" she blurted out.

He grinned at her and adjusted his apron. "You can call me Not Nate. Or maybe the Anti-Nate."

"No. Really," Destiny insisted.

"Harrison," he said, his dark eyes flashing. "Harrison Palmer." He saluted her with the spatula. "And you are . . .

111

wait . . . don't tell me." He studied her, rubbing his chin. "Naomi Watts? I loved you in *The Ring*."

Destiny rolled her eyes. "Ha ha."

"You look a lot like her," Harrison said.

"Yeah. We're both blond and we both have two eyes, a nose, and a mouth," Destiny said. "You'd better start that egg order." She narrowed her eyes at him. "Have you ever done this before?"

He grinned. "Yeah, sure. No problem. Uh . . . just one thing." He held up an egg. "How do you get the yellow part out of this shell thing?"

Destiny laughed. He's funny, she thought. I haven't really laughed in a long time.

She watched him break the eggs on the grill and move them around with the spatula. He's cute too. Tall and broad-shouldered. A great smile. Those big, dark eyes that crinkle up at the sides. Short, brown hair spiked up in the front.

I can't believe Mr. G. forgot to tell me he was starting today.

After the lunch crowd left, she and Harrison had time to chat. She mopped the counter clean while he came out front to help collect plates.

"Good work," she said. "You've done this before."

He shook his head. "No. I bought that book last night. You know, *Fry Cooking for Dummies*."

"No. Really—" she said.

"You have to know where to put that sprig of parsley," he said, dropping a stack of dishes into the dirty dish basket. "Parsley placement. I flunked it twice at cook school."

Destiny laughed. "Aren't you ever serious?"

He didn't answer.

Destiny moved to the back booth and started collecting dirty plates.

"You go to school here?" he asked, motioning out the front window to the campus.

"I'm starting in the fall," Destiny told him. "You?"

He nodded. "Yeah. I finished my first year. Now I'm taking some summer courses. Language stuff. I'm studying Russian."

Destiny turned to look at him. "How come?"

"Beats me." He snickered. "It impresses girls. Are you impressed?"

"Totally," Destiny said. Her face suddenly felt hot.

He's really cute.

"Do you live near here?" she asked.

He nodded. "Yeah, I have an apartment near the campus with a couple of guys. That's why I'm working here, trying to pay the rent. Mr. G. is my stepfather's brother. So he helped me out. Gave me this job."

"Oh. Nepotism," Destiny teased.

"Ooh—big word. You going to be an English major?"

"Probably. Maybe. I don't know."

He laughed. "Luckily, you don't have to decide right away."

"I'm only staying here a year," Destiny told him. "Then

113

I'm transferring out."

"Why didn't you go away to school? Because of the tuition?"

She shrugged. "It's a long story."

You see, my sister became a vampire.

That's a real conversation ender—isn't it?

Harrison picked up the basket of dirty dishes and began lugging it to the kitchen. "Hey, you busy Friday night? My friends and me . . . we're just hanging out at my apartment. Kind of a party. It's my roommate Alby's birthday."

Is he asking me out?

Harrison disappeared into the kitchen. She could hear the dirty plates clattering into the sink.

He's waiting for an answer. Say something, Dee.

I have to get on with my life. Maybe he's just what I need. Someone new. Someone funny and new who doesn't know a thing about me.

She poked her head into the kitchen. "Yeah, sure. Sounds great."

Friday night. As Destiny climbed the narrow staircase to Harrison's apartment, she could hear the party three floors up. Rap music pounded through the stairwell, and she heard laughter and loud voices over the music.

The door to the apartment stood open, and Destiny could see a crowd of young people inside. Two girls sat in the hall with their backs against the wall, smoking and talking. In the corner next to a metal trash can, a tall, blond-haired boy had a girl pressed against the wall, and they were kissing passionately, eyes closed.

Destiny stepped around them and lurched into the doorway. Harrison stood in the middle of the room, talking with a group of guys. He swung around as Destiny entered, and his eyes grew wide, as if he were surprised to see her. He had a Radiohead T-shirt pulled down over faded and torn jeans, a can of Coors in one hand.

"Hey—" he called, pushing his way through the crowd to get to her. "Hi. You made it."

Destiny nodded. "Yeah. Hi. Nice apartment."

Harrison laughed. "You're kidding, right?"

Destiny gazed around the long, L-shaped room. The walls were painted a hideous shade of chartreuse. But a nice, brown leather couch and two La-Z-Boy armchairs were arranged around a big TV screen. A bunch of shouting, cheering guys had jammed onto the couch and chairs and were into an intense PlayStation hockey game.

Two Jimi Hendrix posters were tacked to the wall across from the wide, double windows. Destiny counted five large stereo speakers scattered around the room, all of them booming the new Outkast CD. The speaker tops were cluttered with beer and soda cans and ash trays. A long, aluminum table stood in the alcove of the room. It held two large tubs filled with ice and drinks and open bags of chips.

I've never been in a campus apartment before, Destiny thought. This is totally cool.

Harrison handed her a can of beer. "Hey, want to meet my roomies?"

"Well, yes. You said it's a birthday celebration, right?"

"Yeah. Alby's birthday. You'll like him. He's kinda serious. Like you."

Harrison's words gave Destiny a start. *Is that how he sees me? Kinda serious? Does he think I'm* too *serious?*

"That's Mark over there," Harrison said. He pointed to a very tall, black guy with a shaved head. Dressed in gray sweat pants and a sleeveless, blue T-shirt that showed off his big biceps. He had his arm around a girl at least a foot shorter than he was, and they were laughing hard about something.

Harrison called Mark over and introduced him to Destiny. Mark studied Destiny for a long moment. "Where'd you meet her?" he asked Harrison.

"At the diner."

Mark squeezed Harrison's shoulder and grinned at Destiny. "When you get tired of this loser, come see me— okay?"

Destiny laughed. "For sure."

"Hey, who wants to be in the game?" A short, stocky guy wearing a vintage Bob's Big Boy bowling shirt held up a board game. "We're gonna play Strip Trivial Pursuit. Who wants to play?"

He got a lot of hoots and laughs in reply, but no takers.

Destiny saw some guys watching her from the window. She was wearing a blue-and-white striped top that stopped a couple of inches short of the waist of her jeans. *Guess I* look okay tonight, she thought.

Harrison placed his hand on her back and guided her through the room, introducing her to people. The touch of his hand gave her a shiver.

"Hey, Alby? Where's Alby?" Harrison called.

A tall, lanky guy in black Buddy Holly glasses stepped out of the kitchen, carrying more bags of chips. He had spiky black hair, a silver ring in one ear, and a short, fuzzy beard.

The bags of chips were grabbed away before Alby could set them down on the table. He came up to Destiny and Harrison. "Maybe we should order some pizzas."

"You're the birthday boy," Harrison said. "Order anything you want."

"Hey, thanks."

"As long as *you* pay."

"Hey—nice guy." Alby turned to Destiny and his eyes went wide behind the big, black-framed glasses.

"This is Destiny," Harrison said. "Destiny, Alby."

"Nice to meet you," Destiny said.

Alby stared at her. "We met last night, remember?"

Destiny squinted at him. "I don't think so."

"Yeah. Sure, we did," Alby insisted. "At Club Sixty-One. Remember?"

"Club Sixty-One?" Destiny's mind spun. "No way. I stayed home with my little brother last night."

Alby turned to Harrison. "She has short-term memory loss," he said. "We studied it in Psych last term."

"I was home—" Destiny started.

"We danced. You and me," Alby said. "We had some Jell-O shooters. Remember? You used that fake I.D.? We laughed about that couple that got totally trashed and had to be kicked out? You wore those low-riding jeans."

"Oh, wow." Destiny began to realize what was going on.

And then Alby raised his head, and she saw the spot on his throat. The two pinprick red wounds on his neck.

"Oh, no. Oh, no."

She stared at the cut on Alby's throat—and ran from the room.

chapter twenty

"NOW YOU THINK I'M A PSYCHO NUT"

"I'M SORRY. I CAN'T REALLY EXPLAIN IT," DESTINY said, shaking her head.

Harrison had followed her out into the hall. A couple was still making out by the garbage cans. Through the open doorway, Destiny glimpsed Alby watching her from the middle of the living room, a puzzled expression on his face.

"You . . . don't know why you freaked?" Harrison asked. He squeezed her hand. "Your hand is ice cold. Are you okay? Do you need a doctor or something?"

"No. I'm fine now," Destiny said, heart still pounding like crazy. "I'd better go. I'm really sorry I ran out like that."

He studied her. "You sure you're okay?"

"Yeah. Totally. I just . . . uh . . . I can't explain it."

Actually, I *can* explain it. But you wouldn't believe me,

Harrison. If I told you that Alby ran into my vampire twin sister at the club last night, and she drank his blood, that wouldn't exactly go over, would it?

"You're shaking," Harrison said. "Can I drive you home?"

"No. I . . . brought my car," she replied. "I'll be fine." She forced a smile. "Now you think I'm some kind of psycho nut, don't you?"

He smiled back at her. "Yes, I do. Definitely."

"Great," she muttered, rolling her eyes.

"But I kinda like psycho nuts," Harrison said.

That made her feel a tiny bit better. She leaned forward and gave him a quick peck on the cheek. "See you at work tomorrow." Then she ran down the stairs and out to her car without looking back.

It was a hot, damp night. The steamy air made her cool skin tingle. She fumbled in her bag for her car key. "Where is it? Where is it?"

A wave of panic swept over her.

What did Livvy think she was doing? Except for her family and Ana-Li, everyone thought she had run off to another town with Ross. But now, here she was parading around in the clubs that everyone went to.

Why was she showing herself like that? What were people supposed to think?

Livvy must not care what people think, Destiny decided. She must be so hungry, so desperate for blood she doesn't care if she comes out in the open.

Ari flashed into Destiny's mind. He had been dead for two weeks now, and Destiny thought about him every minute. Such a good, sweet person. He didn't deserve to die that way. Destiny missed him so much.

Livvy is desperate . . . so desperate, she murdered Ari. She didn't give a damn that I cared about him.

A tap on Destiny's shoulder made her cry out in surprise.

She turned and saw a flash of blond hair.

"Livvy?" she gasped. "Ohmigod! Livvy?"

The girl took a step back, her hand still in the air. "Sorry. Didn't mean to startle you."

Not Livvy. An attractive platinum-blond girl with green eyes, dark eyebrows, and dark purple lipstick on her lips. "Is the party in there?" she asked, pointing to Harrison's building.

Still shaken, Destiny nodded. "Yeah. Third floor. You can't miss it."

"Hey, thanks." The girl turned and strode to the building, blond hair waving behind her.

I can't keep doing that, Destiny told herself. I've got to stop seeing Livvy wherever I go.

She drove home, gripping the wheel with both hands, leaning forward in the seat, forcing herself not to think about anything but the driving.

Her cell rang. Ana-Li, she saw. She didn't pick up. I'll call her later when I've calmed down.

Entering her neighborhood, she braked at a stop sign.

She could see Ari's house across the street, windows dark except for his parents' bedroom in the back. A sad house now.

A few minutes later, she pulled the Civic up the drive and stopped a few feet from the garage door. Dad was still not home, she saw. He's worked late every night this week. Mikey and I never see him.

She entered through the front door and saw Mikey jumping up and down on the living room couch. "Hey— what's up?" she called, pushing the door shut behind her. "Where is Mrs. Gilly? Isn't she watching you tonight?"

"She's upstairs. In the bathroom," Mikey said.

Destiny could barely understand him. He had plastic fangs hanging from his mouth, and he wore a black cape over his slender shoulders.

Destiny rushed over to him and hugged him. He pulled free with a growl, snapping at her with the plastic fangs.

"Don't you know any other games?" she asked. "Do you have to play vampire all the time?"

"I'm not playing!" he insisted.

"Mikey, listen to me—"

"I'm not playing. I'm a *real* vampire," he shouted. And then he added, "Just like Livvy."

"But, Mikey—"

"Look," he said. "I'll prove it." He held out his hand.

Destiny gasped as she saw the deep red bite marks up and down his skinny arm.

chapter twenty-one

DAD MIGHT
KILL LIVVY

"DAD, MIKEY IS SERIOUSLY SICK," DESTINY SAID, shaking her head. "And I guess I don't have to tell you it's all Livvy's fault."

Dr. Weller had his elbows on his desk, supporting his chin in his hands. The fluorescent ceiling light reflected in his glasses. "His therapist says he's making progress."

Destiny sighed. She crossed her arms in front of her. "I'm not so sure. You saw his arm. Those bite marks . . ."

"Pretty awful," he agreed. He sat up straight, pulled off the glasses, and rubbed the bridge of his nose. "Mikey has suffered a terrible loss, Dee. We all have. But you and I are a little better equipped to deal with it. He's too young to know how to cope."

A dog howled in the holding pen in the back room, and

that set off all the other dogs yipping and barking.

"We have to stop him from pretending to be a vampire all the time," Destiny said. She shuddered. "It's not helping him."

"And in a way, it might be," her dad said softly. "By playing the role, maybe it helps him work out his fears. Maybe it helps him deal with the frightening thoughts he's having."

Destiny stared at the floor. She didn't know what to say. And she hated seeing her father so sad and tired-looking. He's aged twenty years this summer, she thought.

When she finally looked up, he was crumpling the papers on his desk.

"Dad—what are you doing?"

He angrily ripped the papers in half.

"Dad—?"

"I want to bring Livvy home. I want to restore her to a normal life. Ross, too. But my work is going nowhere, Dee. I . . . I can't find the formula. I've missed time and time again. I'm a failure. We have to face the fact."

Destiny wanted to say something to comfort him. But what could she say?

"So many pressures," he muttered. "So many pressures . . ."

And that's when he told her about the abandoned apartment building near campus. Vampires had been tracked there. Vampires were living there.

"My hunters and I . . . we have to clean the building out,"

he told her. "The pressure is on to take care of the vampire problem in Dark Springs. I'm the leader of the Hunters. I have no choice. My hunters and I have to go in there and kill as many vampires as we can. In two weeks. Sunday at dawn. After the night of the full moon. That's when we'll strike."

All Destiny could think about was Livvy and Ross.

Were they living in that unfinished apartment building too?

Could her father kill his own daughter?

He couldn't—could he?

"I'm sorry to lay this on you," Destiny told Ana-Li. "But I don't have anyone else I can tell."

Ana-Li sighed. "I just came to say good-bye, Dee. I'm leaving tomorrow morning. I . . . I'm so sorry I won't be here to help you."

She wrapped Destiny in a hug.

"I'll e-mail you as soon as I get moved into the dorm. I promise," Ana-Li said, raising one hand as if swearing an oath. "If I can't get my laptop hooked up, I'll call you."

"Thanks," Destiny said, holding onto her friend.

"What about the new boyfriend?" Ana-Li asked. "Can't you confide in him?"

"Harrison? He's been very sweet. And we've been seeing each other just about every night. But . . . I can't tell him about Livvy yet. I just can't. I don't know him well enough."

Ana-Li grinned at her. "But you'd like to know him really well—right?"

"Well . . . yeah. But I can't think about that now." Destiny started to pace back and forth along the room above the garage. She kept staring at Livvy's bed. Livvy's *empty* bed.

"I have to find a way to warn Livvy. Livvy and Ross."

"Even after she was so horrible to you?" Ana-Li asked. "Even after she dragged you off in that parking lot and threatened to drink your blood?"

Destiny stopped pacing. She gripped the back of her desk chair as if holding herself up. "She's my sister," she said through gritted teeth. A tear slid down one cheek. "She's my sister, and I want her back. For her sake. For Mikey's sake. For all of us."

She took a breath and let it out slowly. "But if Dad finds her in that apartment building near campus . . . if Dad finds her . . ." The words caught in her throat.

"He wouldn't drive a stake through Livvy's heart," Ana-Li insisted.

A chill ran down Destiny's back. "He might."

Destiny couldn't sleep that night. Her thoughts swirled round and round until the room spun and her head pounded.

"Dad might kill Livvy."

She pictured her mother, tall and blond and pretty, like her twin daughters. And so young. Destiny only remembered her mother young.

Her mother was bitten by a vampire, a vampire who wanted to take her away, to make her his. She killed herself instead. She killed herself to escape the vampire's clutches.

That's why Dad became leader of the Hunters. That's why he is determined to wipe them out. They took away the love of his life.

And that's why he has been searching for a cure, a formula to restore vampires to a normal life. But he has failed. His daughter is a vampire, and he has failed to find a cure.

And now he will hunt her down. And his hatred for vampires will force him to kill her. If he doesn't do it, one of his hunters will.

Unless I get there first, Destiny thought, rolling onto her side, scrunching the sheet to her chin.

Unless I can warn Livvy.

But how?

After that fight in the club parking lot, I don't think she'll talk to me. If she sees me coming, she'll change into a creature and fly away. If I tell her what Dad and his hunters are planning, she won't believe me. She'll think it's a trick to get her to come home.

So . . . what can I do?

The ceiling spun above Destiny's head. Light and shadows danced crazily, like wild creatures let loose in the room. Somewhere in the distance, a siren wailed.

What can I do?

And then she had an idea.

chapter twenty-two

ONE EVIL DAWN

DESTINY SAT STRAIGHT UP AND KICKED THE COVERS away.

Yes. Yes.

Ross.

Ross will talk to me. Ross always liked me. And he was always easy to talk to.

I'll find Ross. I'll tell him what's going to happen. Then Ross can talk to Livvy. And maybe . . . maybe they'll both be saved.

I'll go at dawn, Destiny decided. When the vampires have been out all night and are falling asleep.

At least I have a plan. I'll go into that building. I'll find Ross. I'll tell him . . . I'll tell him . . .

She settled back down and shut her eyes. But she knew she'd never fall asleep this night.

* * *

At a few minutes before six, she crept silently down the stairs, into the dark kitchen, dishwasher light blinking, and out the back door. Her old Civic refused to start until the third try. She looked to the house to make sure the grinding sounds hadn't awakened her father.

Then she slid the gearshift into drive and headed off, into a gray world, high clouds blocking the rising sun, bare black trees shivering in the cool, morning breeze.

Not many cars on the road. A few sleepy-eyed people on their way to early morning jobs.

Destiny realized she was gritting her teeth so hard, her jaw ached. This is the best time to look for Ross, she assured herself for the hundredth time. The vampires will all be heading in to sleep, weary after a night of prowling.

Will I be able to wake him? Will he recognize me?

Of course he will. He's still Ross.

She drove her car around the campus square. Squirrels scampered over the lawn. The sun still hadn't burned through the clouds.

A few moments later, Destiny pulled the car up to the side of the unfinished apartment building. She climbed out, legs rubbery, heart suddenly pounding. And gazed up the side of the redbrick wall at the rows of open, unglassed windows.

Two large crows stared back at her from a third-floor window ledge. She heard a fluttering sound and saw a bat shoot into a window near the top.

"Oh, wow."

So many apartments, she thought. How will I ever find Ross?

I'll just have to be lucky, she decided. I have to save him and my sister.

Taking a deep breath, she made her way through the front entrance, into the dark lobby. She stepped past rolls of wire and cable and a stack of Sheetrock squares, past the open elevator shaft, and started up the concrete stairs.

Her shoes echoed hollowly in the stairwell. The only sound until she reached the first floor—and heard the moans and sighs and groans of the sleeping vampires. Squinting into the gray light, she gazed in horror at the row of open apartment doorways.

I'll start here, she decided, gripping the railing. I can't call out his name. It would wake everyone up. I'll have to peek into every apartment until I find him.

Her whole body trembling now, she forced herself to move away from the stairs, into the trash-cluttered hall, up to the first door.

I should have brought a flashlight. I thought there would be some sun. The pale, gray light from the hall windows seemed to lengthen the shadows and make everything appear darker.

Sticking her head through the doorless opening, Destiny peered into the dark apartment. She couldn't see anything, but she heard low, steady breathing. She took a step inside. Then one more step.

And in the soupy gray, she saw two girls asleep on their

backs on low cots against the wall, dark hair spread over their pillows, mouths open revealing curled fangs that slid up and down with each breath they took.

Destiny backed into the hall. The next two apartments appeared empty. No furniture. No sounds of sleep.

A long, mournful sigh echoed down the hallway. It sent a shiver down Destiny's back.

She peered into the third apartment. And saw a scrawny, little man asleep on the floor, a pillow under his bald head, his sunken eyes wide open. Destiny gasped and backed away, thinking he could see her. But he was sound asleep.

Moans and harsh snoring followed her to the next apartment. A man and woman, sleeping on a bare mattress, holding hands, their fangs dripping with saliva.

Back into the hall. Nearly at the end now, and no sign of Ross. She stepped around a pile of trash, mostly newspapers and magazines, tossed carelessly against the wall.

The papers rustled. Destiny stopped. What made them move? There was no wind here.

She stared as the papers crinkled. She heard scratching sounds from underneath the pile. "Oh." She uttered a soft cry as two fat rats slithered out.

They turned and gazed up at her, staring for the longest while, as if challenging her.

Her whole body tensed, Destiny backed away. Are these really rats? she wondered. Or are they vampires in rat bodies?

The swooping bat in her living room flashed into her mind. Livvy? Had it been Livvy?

The two rats raised up on their hind legs and took a step toward Destiny. One of them bared its teeth and uttered a shrill hiss.

Destiny wanted to turn and run. But she knew she shouldn't turn her back on the advancing rats.

They stood still now, on their back legs, long, pink tails whipping back and forth, scraping the concrete floor. Their eyes glowed dully like black pearls. They both opened their mouths and uttered warning screeches, furiously waving their front paws up and down in slashing motions.

I have to get away.

Destiny spun away from them, tried to run—and collided full force with a figure standing behind her.

"Hey—!" She stumbled and fell into him, and they both staggered back. Her cheek brushed the rough fabric of his sweater.

"Ross—?" She grabbed his shoulders to pull herself back on her feet, shoulders hard as bone. Not Ross.

"S—sorry," she choked out. "I didn't see you. I was—"

She stared at him. He was good looking. Young. About Destiny's age. Short, dark hair, dark eyes, a thin, straight nose.

Then he turned—and Destiny opened her mouth in a horrified gasp.

The other half of his face—*missing*! The flesh ended in the middle, a line right down the center of his face, giving way to solid skull.

Destiny stared open-mouthed, too horrified to breathe. No eye in the gaping, empty socket, no flesh over the toothless jaw.

Half a face, Destiny saw. Normal looking on one side, even handsome. An eyeless skull on the other half.

Trembling, Destiny tried to back away.

"What's wrong?" he whispered. His teeth clicked as he talked, and his single eye rolled around in its socket. "Don't be frightened. Don't worry. I'll save my *good* side for you, babe."

He grabbed her. Circled his arms tightly around her. Arms like bones—and powerful, clamping her to him.

"No, please—"

She couldn't breathe.

He held her so tightly, her ribs ached. Her chest felt about to burst.

He lowered his face to her. She could see both sides at once now, the skeleton and the good-looking face. Both grinning at her coldly, half-lips pulled back so she could see his teeth.

He pressed his lips to hers.

Ohh. She felt soft flesh and bone.

Her stomach heaved.

He pulled his mouth away quickly, single eye flashing.

And then she saw the fangs, yellow and curled, slide down from his open mouth.

"So sweet, so sweet," he whispered, sour breath washing over her, making her choke. And then he sank the disgusting fangs into her throat.

chapter twenty-three

"I WANT TO GO BACK TO MY OLD LIFE"

SHE FELT A STAB OF PAIN.

Then heard a loud shout.

"GET AWAY FROM HER!"

The vampire seemed to spin to the voice. But then Destiny realized someone had pulled him off her. Another vampire, face hidden in shadow, had grabbed him by the shoulders.

"First come, first served," the half-faceless one said softly, teeth clicking. He tensed his body as if preparing for a fight.

"I don't think so," the other replied.

And then they flung themselves at each other. Growling, cursing, they wrestled from one side of the hall to the other, smashing each other against the concrete walls.

Gasping for breath, Destiny felt the pinprick wounds in her neck as she tried to back away to safety.

They're fighting over which one gets me, she realized. Frozen in horror, she watched the battle.

Their cries and shouts had awakened others, who stood in the dark doorways all down the hall, staring in silence as the two vampires slashed at each other, shoving and biting.

I'm pinned here, Destiny thought. I can't run. If I do, the others will get me.

She backed into a corner, hands pressed against the sides of her face, still gasping for breath.

Fighting over me . . .

Fighting to see who gets to drink my blood . . .

With his back to Destiny, the new arrival hoisted up the half-faced vampire by the waist, lifted him high over his head and, with a powerful heave, tossed him out an open window.

Destiny heard the vampire's scream as he fell down the side of the building. Down . . . down . . . And then the scream was replaced by an angry bird cry, which rose up until Destiny could see a hawk, wings spread wide, through the window, sailing up, turning and taking one last glance at her, then floating away.

And now the winner of the battle, panting noisily, brushing his wet hair off his face, turned to claim his prize. He lurched toward Destiny arms outstretched . . .

. . . And Destiny recognized him. "Ross—!" she screamed. "Ross—it's me!"

His mouth dropped open. He wiped sweat from his eyes—and squinted at her in the inky light. "Destiny—?"

"Yes. Yes, it's me!"

"Whoa." He was still breathing hard, chest heaving up and down. He had deep scratch marks on one side of his neck, and a red welt had formed under one eye.

"I don't believe it," he said, shaking his head hard. Then he lurched forward and wrapped her in a hug. "Dee, I'm so glad to see you."

Destiny let out a sigh of relief. It *is* the same Ross, she thought.

She gazed over his shoulder and saw eyes staring at them in doorways all down the hall, cold faces, angry and frightening.

"Can we . . . go somewhere?" she whispered.

Ross took her by the hand and led her to the stairway. He helped her up the steep, concrete steps to the second floor. Then he led the way to a small apartment halfway down the hall.

The clouds had finally started to burn away, and morning sunlight peeked into the open window. Destiny hugged herself. The room still had the chill of night.

She glanced around quickly. A pile of clothes, mostly jeans and T-shirts, in one corner. A couch with one cushion missing. A metal folding chair. A clock radio on the floor. The only furnishings.

Ross led her over to the couch. "Dee, I can't believe you're here. I'm so happy to see you," he said. He motioned for her to sit down. Then he dropped down beside her, sweeping his hair back with both hands.

He's changed, Destiny thought, studying him. He used to have that spark in his eyes, that flash of fire. But it's gone. He looks so tired . . . exhausted. And not because of the fight with the other vampire.

"How are you?" he asked. "How's Mikey? And your dad?"

"Not great," Destiny replied. "It's been really hard with Livvy gone. I mean, it's hard to explain to yourself why—"

"Livvy," Ross interrupted, shaking his head. "Livvy. Livvy. She's hard to figure, you know?"

"I . . . saw her the other night," Destiny continued, the words catching in her throat. "She was so horrible to me, Ross. Like she *hated* me. And what did I do to her? Nothing. I only wanted to talk with her."

"She's gotten weird," Ross said, lowering his head. "This was supposed to be so exciting. You know. Livvy and me. Living forever and everything. She promised. She promised me it would be awesome. But now . . ." He glanced to the window. "Now she usually doesn't want to hang with me. She's got new friends that she cares about."

Destiny nodded. She didn't know what to say. "Ross—?"

He kept his eyes down at the floor. "I'm so unhappy," he said finally. "I mean, this life is so hard. I wish . . . I wish I'd never followed Livvy."

"I'm sorry too," Destiny murmured.

"She likes it. I really think she does," he continued,

finally turning to face her. "I don't understand it. But I think Livvy enjoys the excitement. You know, the adventure. She likes the . . . *badness* of it. And the idea that she never has to grow old."

Destiny nodded. "When she was little, her favorite cartoon was *Peter Pan*. You know. The Disney one. Now I guess she liked it because Peter and the Lost Boys never grew up, either.

"I don't know why I went with her," Ross said. He climbed to his feet and moved to the window. He leaned on the sill, keeping his back to the rising sunlight as he spoke. "It was crazy. I guess I went a little nuts or something. But now . . ."

He swallowed. "Now I'd give anything to have my old life back. I mean it, Dee. Anything. I'm so unhappy. I just want to see my sister again . . . and Mom and Dad. I just want—"

"Maybe it can happen," Destiny interrupted.

He squinted at her. "Why? Has your dad—?"

"No. He hasn't found anything. Not yet. But he's working on it, Ross. He won't quit till he finds a cure."

"That's great," Ross said. "I don't know how much more I can take. Really."

Destiny climbed to her feet and hugged herself tightly. "Listen, Ross, I came here for a reason. I came to warn you. The Hunters are going to come. They know about this place. They're going to kill as many vampires as they can."

Ross nodded. He didn't seem surprised. "We knew

they'd come after us sooner or later."

"You and Livvy have got to get out," Destiny said. "You've got to talk to her, Ross. She won't talk to me."

He scratched his head. "I . . . I'll try."

Destiny could feel her emotions tightening her throat. "You've got to tell her," she said. "You've got to tell her to get away from here. Maybe you can convince her, Ross. Have you told her you want to give up the vampire life? Maybe you can convince her too."

Ross hesitated. "I don't think so. Whenever I start to talk about it . . ." His voice trailed off in a sigh.

Destiny felt tears rolling down her cheeks. She didn't make any attempt to stop them. "Tell her. Tell her, Ross."

Ross nodded. "I'll see what I can do. Really. I'll try, Dee."

A sob escaped Destiny's throat. Tears blurred her vision. "Tell her I still love her," she choked out. "Tell her I'll do anything to have her back."

And then she ran, out the door of the shabby apartment and down the long hallway . . . ran away from this world of darkness . . . back to her own life.

chapter twenty-four

A DEATH IN
THE VAMPIRE FAMILY

IS THAT DESTINY?

Yes, of course it is.

Livvy hid behind a trash Dumpster and watched her sister run from the apartment building. Destiny dropped her bag, picked it up, then fumbled inside it for her car key.

What is she doing here so early? Livvy wondered. The sun is just coming up. Did she come to see me? Does she still think if she begs hard enough, I'll come home?

She watched Destiny stumble over a pile of broken bricks, then run to the side of the building. Destiny had such a distressed look on her face, Livvy felt a pang of guilt.

I didn't want to cause you so much sadness, Dee. What I did wasn't about you at all. It was about me. But you can't accept that, can you? Because everything—*everything*—

always had to be about you.

Destiny pulled open her car door and plunged inside.

You must have sneaked out of the house before dawn, Livvy thought. Now why would you pay me a visit at this hour? Do you think I know something about Ari? Is that it?

Think I know something about how poor Ari died? Well, Dee, you've got that right.

I do know about Ari. It was my stupid friend Monica. I warned her to be careful, to go slowly, a few sips at a time. But Monica never knows when to stop. She always wants more more more.

Suzie and I both got on her case when she told us she'd killed Ari. "I couldn't help it," Monica said. "I was so hungry, and I lost track. It was an accident. Really."

Accidents happen, right?

No way.

Not when it gets the whole town excited and upset. And the police. Monica should know better. She risked all of us for one night of pleasure. She's my friend, but she's also a stupid cow.

And yes, I felt bad about Ari. I mean, he was a geeky guy, totally clueless. Spending all his time on horror movies and *Star Trek* websites. But he was smart and funny too. And I know you really liked him.

Whatever.

It's done, okay. He's history.

So why did you come to see me this morning? To hear about how Ari died? How would that help you? It won't bring the poor guy back.

Livvy watched Destiny's car pull away, tires squealing. Again, she pictured the distressed look on her sister's face.

Sorry, Dee. I really am. But get over it.

Don't come here begging me to give up my new life.

Livvy licked her lips. Mmmm. A trace of the sweet blood lingered there.

That Alby is a good guy, she thought, shutting her eyes for a moment. Such sweet blood, almost like dessert. I'm going to bring him along slowly, so slowly he won't even notice.

The morning sun spread an orange glow around the apartment building. Livvy squinted at the brightening light.

I'd better get inside. The sun burns my eyes. I don't have my shades.

She started toward the front door—then stopped.

Whoa. Hold on. Maybe Dee didn't come to see me.

Livvy bit her bottom lip, new thoughts flashing through her mind.

Maybe Dee came to see Ross.

Maybe she came at dawn hoping to find him without me around.

Has she been seeing Ross all along? Destiny always had a thing for him. I think she was really jealous when Ross decided he liked me better.

When Ross decided he loved me . . .

But Ross is so eager to connect to his old life. He begged me to let him see his family in line at the movie theater. Has he also been trying to get together with my sister?

Livvy darted into the darkness of the building. As she climbed the stairs, she could hear the groans and sighs of the sleeping vampires.

But she didn't feel the least bit sleepy. She had to get to the bottom of this.

Her shoes thudded the concrete floor as she ran down the long, narrow hallway toward Ross's apartment. She edged past a stack of Sheetrock, then a pile of old newspapers.

Ross, please don't tell me you've been seeing Destiny. Please tell me she came to see *me*.

She stopped at the open doorway to Ross's apartment to catch her breath. Then she burst inside.

"Ross—?"

It took her eyes a few moments to adjust to the bright light that washed into the room from the window. Then Livvy spotted Ross—and she opened her mouth and screamed in horror.

"Ross? Nooooooo! Oh, no! Please   NOOOOOOOOO!"

chapter twenty-five

"IT WON'T BE PRETTY"

LIVVY STAGGERED OVER TO ROSS'S BODY. SPRAWLED on his back on the floor. Legs spread. Hands raised, still gripping the wooden stake pushed through his chest.

Wooden stake . . .

Livvy gaped at the stake, a plank of light wood. The kind of wood scattered all over this unfinished building.

The stake had been driven through Ross's T-shirt, through the center of his chest. Through his heart.

And now he lay with his eyes wide open, blank, glassy . . . wide open . . . wide open as if still staring up at his attacker.

His head tilted to one side. His mouth hung open in a silent scream. Hands still gripping the stake.

"Ross—" Livvy uttered his name as she dropped down beside his lifeless body. "Oh, no, Ross. Oh, no."

Murdered.

She cradled his head in her arms.

Murdered. His body still warm.

And yes, she knew . . .

Holding onto the boy who had cared enough about her to follow her . . . the boy who had loved her so much, he became a vampire just to be with her. Holding onto Ross's lifeless head, Livvy knew who had murdered him.

Destiny.

She had seen Destiny running from the building. In such a hurry to get away.

Destiny came at dawn, sneaked into the building to kill Ross.

And why?

Cradling Ross's head, Livvy shut her eyes and thought hard.

Why?

To pay me back for deserting the family.

No.

Oh, wait. I get it. I totally get it. That was Destiny's way of paying me back for Ari.

Destiny thinks I killed Ari. So she paid me back by killing Ross.

Poor, sweet, innocent Ross.

Could Destiny really do this? Is she angry enough? Desperate enough? Crazy enough?

Yes. I saw her face as she ran from the building.

I saw the tears running down her cheeks. Saw the wild

look in her eyes. The fear mixed with anger. Mixed with hatred.

She hates me so much, she murdered the boy who loved me.

With a long howl of sorrow, Livvy hugged Ross's lifeless head, pressed it to her, ran her hands through his hair one last time.

"You can't get away with this, Destiny," she said out loud in a cold, hard voice. "I'll find a way to pay you back. Yes, I will. And it won't be pretty."

chapter twenty-six

"I'D LIKE TO TEAR DESTINY TO BITS"

SOBBING NOW, LIVVY GENTLY LOWERED ROSS'S HEAD to the floor. She climbed unsteadily to her feet, pulled a blanket off his narrow cot, and covered his body with it, tugging the ends of the blanket around the wooden stake.

Livvy's whole body shuddered.

What must that feel like? To have a sharpened wooden stake shoved through your chest into your heart?

She couldn't imagine the agony Ross must have felt. The pain from the puncture. Waves of pain shooting through his body like electric currents . . . as he realized . . . realized he was about to lose his life.

She grabbed her own chest. She suddenly felt as if she couldn't take another breath.

I have to get out of here.

Still holding her chest, she turned away from Ross and stumbled to the door. She started to breathe again out in the hall. And then she climbed the stairs and ran to her room, shoes thudding noisily . . . How wonderful to be able to make a noise, to be alive, to run . . . Ross will never run again . . . never.

Sunshine poured in through the open window. She fumbled on her dresser top until she found her sunglasses. Slipped them on, blinking, heart thudding, two pictures remaining in her mind.

Two pictures refusing to fade . . .

Ross dead on the floor, his hands—his beautiful hands—gripping the wooden stake that killed him.

And Destiny running from the apartment building, tears running down her cheeks, her expression so angry, so upset.

Livvy paced back and forth in the small, nearly bare living room, her hands balled into tight fists. The anger boiled up in her until she felt ready to explode.

I'd like to follow Dee home right now, she thought. Burst in at breakfast and drag her away. Slash her, tear her to bits with my own hands.

Oh, wow. Could I do that? Could I do that to Dad and Mikey?

Maybe. It's not like I was ever appreciated at home. Or like anyone tried to understand me. Destiny was always the princess. And I was always . . . trouble.

Well, I tried to escape all that. I tried to escape my

family. I tried to do them a favor. Go away so I wouldn't be trouble anymore.

So why couldn't my sister leave things alone?

Stay home and be the good twin, Dee. Stay with Dad and Mikey and be the princess.

Don't come here and kill someone I really care about.

She could feel the anger rising again, feel all her muscles tensing. And then suddenly, she felt as if she weighed a thousand pounds.

So weary.

Out all night, and then come home to such horror.

She yawned. I need to sleep. Sleep will help me think more clearly. I can make a plan. I can—

She heard a scraping sound from the other room. Footsteps.

"Monica? Suzie? Are you in here?"

No answer.

Livvy stared at the doorway to the bedroom. She took a few steps. "Who's in there?"

And as she stared, a figure stepped out of the shadows. He smiled at her.

"You?" Livvy cried. "What are *you* doing in here?"

chapter twenty-seven

BLOOD ON
HER LIPS

PATRICK CAME TOWARD HER SLOWLY, HANDS IN THE pockets of his black denim jeans. His dark eyes locked on hers. As his grin widened, she saw the dimples in his cheeks—and remembered the way he smiled at her at the dance club.

"How long have you been here? What are you doing here?" she asked.

He shrugged. "Just waiting for you."

Livvy rushed to him. "Oh, Patrick. I'm so glad to see you. Something . . . something *terrible* has happened."

His smile faded quickly. "What is it? Are you okay?"

"No. No, I'm not. I . . . I . . ." She grabbed his arm and pulled him out of the apartment. "You've got to see. I . . . I'm so upset."

She pulled him through the hall, then down the stairs to Ross's apartment. They stepped through a square of bright sunlight on the floor, to the back of the apartment, to the body covered by a purple blanket, wooden stake poking straight up into the air.

"Here," Livvy said, trembling. She tugged away the blanket.

Patrick gasped and bent to examine Ross's body closer. "Oh, no," he murmured. "I don't believe this."

Angrily, he grabbed the stake in both hands and ripped it from Ross's chest. Then he flung it against the bedroom wall, where it hit and clattered to the bare floor.

He turned to Livvy, his features tight with anger. "Who did this? We can't let them get away with this."

"He . . . was my friend," Livvy said in a whisper. "He was a good guy. He . . ."

Patrick leaned his back against the wall and brushed a hand through his long, brown hair. "Murdered in his own apartment," he murmured. "He was your friend?"

Livvy nodded, tears running down her cheeks.

He raised his eyes to her and studied her. "When did this happen? Do you have any idea who did it?"

Livvy hesitated.

Yes, I have an idea who did it.

But I can't tell him.

I can't turn my sister over to him so easily. I want to handle her myself. I want to make Destiny pay for what she did. I don't want someone else to get the revenge *for* me.

"No. I don't have a clue," Livvy said, lowering her eyes to the floor. "It probably happened this morning. I'm sure Ross was out all night. His body . . . his face . . . it was still warm when I came in here."

Patrick narrowed his eyes at her. "Do you always come in to see him early in the morning?"

"Uh . . . no," Livvy replied. "Not usually."

"Well then, why did you come to his apartment this morning?" Patrick asked.

He sounded suspicious. Livvy didn't like the question.

"I wanted to ask him something. I wanted to ask Ross if he knew a guy I met last night." A total lie. Was Patrick buying it?

He seemed to. He scratched his head. "And you can't think of anyone who had a grudge against Ross? Who might've wanted revenge or something? No enemies? You were his friend, Livvy. No one comes to mind?"

She shook her head. "No. No one." She glanced down at the body and let out a sob. "I . . . I'm really going to miss him."

Patrick crossed the room quickly and wrapped Livvy in a hug. She pressed her hot, damp cheek against his. He tightened his arms around her waist.

It felt good to be held by someone, someone solid and strong.

Livvy raised her face to his and kissed him. She wrapped her hands around the back of his neck and held his head as they kissed.

"Mm." She let out a sound as she felt his teeth bite into her lips. He pressed his mouth against hers, and she felt a shock of pain.

Suddenly, he ended the kiss. He pulled his face away, then lowered it to hers again—and licked the blood off her lips.

Livvy realized she was breathing hard, her heart racing. For the first time in her life, she felt dizzy from a kiss.

Patrick held her tightly, licking the top lip clean, then the bottom. When he backed away, he had her blood on his lips.

"I'll see you later," he said, and vanished from the room.

"Yeah. Later," she repeated. She stood unsteadily, eyes clamped shut, waiting for her heart to stop racing. And then . . . she thought about Destiny.

Destiny, who had murdered Ross.

chapter twenty-eight

LIVVY'S
REVENGE

A FEW DAYS LATER, UNABLE TO FORGIVE DESTINY, unable to control her rage, Livvy found the Four Corners Diner. Peering through the front window, she saw Destiny behind the counter.

Seeing her sister working so calmly, so normally, as if nothing had happened . . . as if she hadn't murdered someone who'd been close to them both . . . made Livvy boil with anger.

What can I do? How can I pay her back for this?

What could she have been thinking? How could Destiny hate me *so much* that she would murder Ross?

Heart pounding, Livvy made her way to the back of the restaurant. Then she used her powers to transform into a tiny, white mouse.

Down on all fours, she found a crack in the back wall. She squeezed through it, into the kitchen. Creeping along the molding, Livvy moved silently toward the front. The aroma of frying eggs and bacon made her stand up and sniff the air with her pink nose.

As she stood up, the young man behind the fry grill came into view. Very nice looking, Livvy thought. Check out those big, brown eyes. And he looks like he works out.

He turned away from the grill. Livvy ducked under a cabinet.

"Tuna salad on whole wheat," Destiny called from the front. "And Harrison, are you working on that cheese-burger rare?"

So his name is Harrison, Livvy told herself.

She started to feel hungry. Not from the smell of the food frying on the grill—but from the look of Harrison's broad shoulders, those eyes that crinkled at the corners, that long neck, the perfect throat . . .

She let out a soft squeak.

Oh, wow. Control yourself, Livvy. Did he hear you? She pressed tighter under the cabinet.

Why did I come here? She wondered, staring up at Harrison.

To spy on Destiny, of course. To see her face, the face of a murderer. Why? Well . . . Because . . . Because . . .

I'm not sure.

I'm so confused and upset, I can't think straight.

Destiny appeared in the kitchen, carrying a stack of

dirty dishes. She dropped them into a basket on the sink counter.

"Whew." She wiped her forehead with the back of her hand, then washed her hands in the sink. Livvy watched her walk over to Harrison.

"How's it going?" Destiny put a hand on Harrison's shoulder.

"Not bad," he replied, scraping the grill. "Want some eggs or something? A little lunch break?"

"No, thanks. Check this out." She held up a coin. "A quarter. That table of four—they tipped me a quarter."

Harrison stared at it. "You and I split that, right? When do I get my share?"

They both laughed. The quarter fell from Destiny's hand and rolled onto the floor.

Then Livvy watched them kiss, a long, tender kiss.

And she knew what she wanted to do.

Harrison is my guy. This is going to be so *sweet*.

Destiny, dear, let's see how eager you are to kiss your lovely Harrison after I turn him into a vampire!

part six

chapter twenty-nine

THE PARTY CRASHER

"I THINK YOU'RE DEFINITELY HELPING MIKEY," Destiny said.

Harrison shrugged. "I didn't do anything."

"He responds to you," she replied. "He likes you. I mean, you got him to come out of the Bat Cave—his room—and actually throw a Frisbee around in the backyard. That was an amazing accomplishment."

"Yeah, true," Harrison agreed. "That poor guy seemed so stressed out when he got outside. Until I made him chase after the Frisbee a few times, he was shaking like a leaf. He kept gazing up at the sky, checking out the tree limbs. I don't know what he expected to find up there."

He expected to find Livvy, Destiny thought.

But Harrison doesn't know that.

She told Harrison that Mikey had a lot of problems because their mother had died so suddenly. She hadn't told Harrison anything about Livvy. He didn't even know she had a twin sister.

Destiny felt her throat tighten. She had been thinking about Livvy. *Did Ross talk to her? Did he pass on my message to her?*

It had been three days, and she hadn't heard from Ross or her sister.

Destiny chewed her bottom lip. *Should I go back there and talk to Ross again? Was sneaking over there at dawn a waste of time? Is Livvy just going to ignore my visit?*

Harrison pulled the car to the curb. Destiny slid down the visor and checked her lipstick in the mirror. She gazed out at the row of townhouses, aging three-story buildings—paint peeling and shingles missing—that had been turned into apartments for community college students.

Lights blazed in the front windows of the house on the right. And Destiny could hear rap music blaring without even opening the car door.

"Do I look okay?" she asked. She wore a light blue tank top, baggy, white shorts, and flip-flops. It was a steamy hot July night and she wanted to be comfortable.

Harrison smiled and nodded. "Awesome."

He started to open his door, then stopped. "Are you getting tired of these crowded, noisy parties?"

"No way," Destiny said without having to think about it. "I'm meeting some nice people. And it kinda makes me feel like I'm already part of the scene. You know. Like I'm already in college."

She climbed out of the car and straightened her shirt. She saw groups of young people on the grass in front of the building. Several sat on the stoop, cans of beer in their hands. Two large golden Labs with red bandannas around their necks chased each other across the street and back.

Harrison took her hand and they walked up the stoop, stepping around two girls on the steps who were smoking—both talking heatedly at once—and into Harrison's friend's apartment.

Destiny stepped into the big, smoky front room, filled with people her age in shorts and jeans, sprawled over the furniture, standing in clumps, shouting over the deafening music. She recognized some girls she met at Alby's birthday party and hurried over to say hi to them.

Livvy was always the party person, she thought. But I'm starting to enjoy them more. Maybe because I'm older now—and being out of high school makes *everyone* more relaxed.

Harrison introduced her to Danny, his best friend from high school. He was a short, stocky guy, kind of funny-looking with tiny, round eyes on top of a bulby nose, and thick, steel wool hair standing up on his head.

He and Harrison walked off talking, and Destiny crossed the room to get a Coke. She ran into Alby at the food table, and they hung out for a while.

Destiny tried not to stare at the bandage on Alby's

neck. But it made her very uncomfortable. She made an excuse and hurried away.

People were scattered all over the townhouse, and Destiny gave herself a tour. Wish I could live away from home, she thought. The fun of college is being away from home, living on your own for the first time.

But why even think about it? No way she could leave Dad and Mikey now.

She returned to the front room and talked to some people she'd met at the diner. A couple of guys hit on her, and she brushed them off easily.

After a while, she realized she hadn't seen Harrison for a long time. She glanced at her watch. She hadn't seen him for at least half an hour.

Weird.

Destiny gazed around the room. Harrison, where are you?

She saw Alby in the corner with a skinny, red-haired girl a foot taller than him, and made her way through the crowd to him. "Have you seen Harrison?" She had to shout over the loud voices and the booming rap music.

Alby shook his head. "No. Not for a while. Do you know Lily?"

No. Destiny didn't know Lily. She stayed and talked to her for a while. She kept expecting Harrison to appear at her side, but—no sign of him.

She searched the back rooms and the kitchen, piled high with garbage and empty beer and soda cans. He's got to be here somewhere, she thought.

Doesn't he wonder where I am?

Destiny returned to her spot in front of the fireplace in the living room. A few minutes later, Harrison turned from the drinks table, spotted her, and his eyes went wide, as if he was surprised to see her there.

He carried two cans of Coors and hurried over to her. "Here's the beer you wanted," he said. "How'd you get back here so fast?"

Destiny stared at him. "Excuse me? I didn't ask you for a beer."

He crinkled up his face, confused. "Of course, you did. Outside on the stoop, you—"

"Huh? Outside?"

Destiny's heart leaped up to her throat. She narrowed her eyes at Harrison, her mind spinning.

Outside.

He was talking to me outside on the stoop.

But no. No. It wasn't me.

Livvy!

chapter thirty

LIVVY
AND HARRISON

DESTINY HANDED THE BEER BACK TO HARRISON AND took off. She heard him shouting to her, but she didn't turn around.

Livvy is here. On the front stoop.

Did Ross talk to her? Did he convince her to come see me?

She bumped into a couple leaning on the wall by the door who had their arms around each other, cheeks pressed together. They both let out startled cries as Destiny pushed past them.

"Sorry," she called.

She pushed the screen door open and burst out onto the stoop. "Livvy? Are you here?" she called.

A blond girl in a red halter top and jeans spun toward Destiny.

"Livvy—?"

No.

Destiny ran down the steps onto the grass. The sun had gone down. The moon floated low in a clear, purple sky dotted with stars.

The people on the lawn were all shadows. A few couples were lying in the grass, wrapped up in each other. A circle of guys down near the sidewalk were singing a Beatles song at the top of their lungs.

"Livvy? Are you here?"

Destiny cupped her hands around her mouth and shouted. "Livvy? Livvy?"

No. No answer. Gone.

But she had been here. Harrison had talked to her. And thought he was talking to Destiny.

Did she do that deliberately? Did Livvy come here to trick Harrison? Was it some kind of joke she was playing on Destiny?

Destiny gazed around the front lawn. Music boomed from the open windows. "Livvy? Livvy? Please?"

Then Destiny saw the bat. It fluttered off a slender tree near the curb and flapped slowly toward her. Eyes glowing, the bat swooped low over her head, then spun away and floated toward the street.

Heart pounding, Destiny turned and chased after it.

The bat floated slowly, low to the ground, its wings spread wide, gliding easily. Destiny ran under it, reaching for it with both hands, calling her sister's name breathlessly.

"Livvy, stop! Please—!"

The bat swooped away, just out of her reach.

Running hard, Destiny made another grab for the bat—and missed.

"Ohh—!" Destiny let out a cry as she ran full force into the side mirror of a parked car. The mirror hit her chest. Pain shot through her ribs. She staggered back.

She raised her eyes in time to see the bat vanish into the inky night sky.

Livvy, why did you come? she wondered. If you didn't want to talk to me, what were you doing here?

chapter thirty-one

"YOU'RE STILL CONNECTED TO YOUR SISTER"

LIVVY SWOOPED TO THE SIDE OF THE ABANDONED apartment building, fluttered high against the wall, then dropped gently onto the sill of a glassless window. The night air felt cool on her wings. For a moment, she thought she might turn around and fly out again, fly away from her troubled thoughts, cover herself in the darkness above the trees.

But no. She changed her mind and scuttled inside, shutting her eyes and willing herself to change back to the body that was familiar to her—and unfamiliar at the same time.

Here I am, Livvy Weller once again. Only I'm not really Livvy Weller. I'm someone else, someone new.

She took a deep breath. It always took a while for her heartbeats to slow from the racing rhythm of a bat's heart.

And it took a minute or two for her eyes to adjust to normal, for the night vision to fade, for her hearing to return.

Livvy reached for the floor lamp she had found on the street. Would it work? The electrical generator downstairs was usually broken. She clicked it, and a triangle of pale, yellow light washed over the floor.

"Oh." She blinked as Patrick climbed up from the floor, dusted off the seat of his faded jeans, torn at both knees, and slowly ambled over to her.

She laughed. "Don't you ever knock?"

He grinned, showing those dimples, and pointed behind him. "No door."

She kissed him on the cheek. His skin felt cool and smooth.

"Where've you been?" he asked.

She gave him a sexy smile. "Like it's *your* business?"

"Yes, it is my business," he said, smile fading. He swept a hand back through his dark hair. It had been brushed straight back, but now he'd messed it up. "I . . . I'm interested in you, Liv. I like you, okay? So I want to make sure you don't mess up."

She narrowed her eyes at him. "Mess up? Mess up what?"

He shrugged. "Everything."

Livvy ran her finger down the side of his cheek. "What are you talking about?"

"Where were you tonight?" he asked again.

"Out flying around," she said. "You know. The usual."

He turned those dark, deep eyes on her, and she could feel their power. "You're lying, Liv. Why would you lie to me unless you knew you were out looking for trouble tonight?"

Livvy stared back at him. Was he hypnotizing her or something? Using his powers to invade her mind?

She turned away, but she could still feel the strange power of his stare.

"You went to your sister's party," Patrick said. "You pretended to be your sister, and you fooled her boyfriend, that guy Harrison."

Livvy let out a groan. "I don't believe this. So you're *spying* on me?"

He nodded. "Yes. Why did you do it, Liv? Explain that to me."

Livvy shrugged. "I don't know. I . . . I just don't know. For fun, maybe."

Patrick shook his head. He crossed the room to her. "You didn't do it for fun. You did it because you're still connected to your sister."

"Connected? What the hell is that supposed to mean?" Livvy snapped.

"You've chosen a new life, right?" Patrick asked. "You're one of us now. But you're not really here yet, Liv. You're not whole."

"Not whole?"

"You won't be whole as long as you have a soft spot in your heart."

Livvy stared at him, hands on her waist. "You mean for Destiny? Listen—"

"Your heart still beats for your sister," Patrick said. "You still care about her."

He's wrong, Livvy told herself. I hate Destiny. Hate her! She killed Ross.

"You're crazy," she snapped at Patrick. "I just went to that party to mess with Destiny's mind."

"But, why?" Patrick demanded. "See? You've proven my point, Liv. Why did you go to mess with Destiny's mind? Why did you go to that party? Because you still care about her. You still care what she thinks."

"That is *so* wrong," Livvy insisted.

Patrick softened his tone. "You know I'm right. Admit it. Admit it."

"Stop trying to push me around," Livvy said.

"Listen to me," he said. He wrapped his arms around her. "Listen to me," he repeated, whispering the words now. "You want to be immortal?"

"Of course."

"Then you have to break all ties with the other world."

"I . . . I don't know if I can do that."

"Well then, you have no choice. Don't you see, Livvy? Don't you see the answer? You will never truly be an immortal—*until your sister is one of us!*"

chapter thirty-two

A DATE
WITH A VAMPIRE

"DESTINY A VAMPIRE TOO?" LIVVY STARED HARD AT Patrick. "Yes. I like that idea."

The perfect revenge for what Destiny did to Ross, Livvy thought. Why didn't I think of it?

Maybe I do still care too much about her. Maybe that's why I didn't imagine a revenge this good.

"Yes," she told Patrick. "You might be right. Destiny would be much better off as a vampire. And then I wouldn't have to think about her, about my family back home."

"I knew you'd agree," Patrick said, sitting down on the window ledge, gazing up at the nearly full moon. "Most people finally agree with me."

"It's not like you're an egotist or anything," Livvy said.

He laughed. "I like you, Liv. I really do. And I think I'm

really going to like your sister too."

Livvy narrowed her eyes at him. "Like Destiny? What do you mean?"

"I'll go after Destiny myself and turn her into an immortal. You take care of the new boyfriend. Harrison Palmer." He grinned. "You'll enjoy that, right?"

Livvy nodded. "It won't be hard work. I already spent time with Harrison at that party tonight. We hit it off really well. And he didn't have a clue I wasn't Destiny."

"Excellent!" Patrick rubbed his hands together. "A little project for the two of us."

He wrapped his arms around her waist in a tight hug. Then he kissed her hard, grinding his teeth against her lips until she cried out in pain—and in pleasure.

Destiny arrived at the diner and found Mr. G. behind the grill. "Where's Harrison?" she asked, sliding behind the counter.

"Some kind of mix-up at school," Mr. G. shouted over the crackling and hissing of the eggs and bacon. "He had to go straighten it all out. Don't look for him today. Once you go in that administration building, they don't let you out."

Destiny went to work, clearing dirty dishes off tables, refilling coffee cups, taking orders. Breakfast was the busiest part of the day. A lot of the professors, instructors, and other college workers stopped here before heading to their offices.

"I asked for rye toast, not white."

"Could you top this cup off for me. No—decaf. Make sure it's decaf."

"I asked for *extra* crisp bacon. Look at these soggy things."

Breakfast was the busiest time—and the most difficult.

Destiny wondered what kind of trouble Harrison was having. He hadn't mentioned anything to her at the party last night.

The party . . .

Luckily, Harrison hadn't seen her chase after the bat. If he had, he'd think she was totally nuts!

And of course she didn't tell him he'd spent half an hour talking with her vampire twin. If Harrison knew the truth, he'd freak.

He's a great guy, Destiny thought. I wish I could confide in him. Tell him everything. But I don't want to lose him . . .

A young man leaned over the counter, staring at her.

She shook her head hard, forcing away her troubled thoughts. "Sorry. I didn't see you there." She wiped her hands off on a towel, picked up a menu, and carried it over to him.

He smiled. He had the cutest dimples in his cheeks. Dark eyes, very round and wide, dark hair brushed straight back over his broad forehead. "You were off on some other planet," he said.

She handed him the menu. "Just daydreaming. How long were you watching me?"

He shrugged. "A little while. You look like someone I know."

She studied him. "Oh, really? Are you from Dark Springs?"

"No. Not really. I mean, I am now. I teach across the street. I'm a teaching assistant. For Professor Clark. Heard of him?"

"No. Sorry. I'm starting there this fall. What do you teach?"

"English. Creative writing, actually." He lowered his eyes to the menu.

"I'm very into creative writing," Destiny said. "Maybe I'll be in your class sometime."

He smiled. Again those dimples. "I'd like that."

How old was he? Maybe twenty? Except his eyes looked older somehow.

He stuck out his hand. "My name is Patrick."

She reached over the counter to shake it. "Destiny Weller. Do you know what you want?"

He eyed her meaningfully. "I'm thinking about it." He held onto her hand for the longest time.

Destiny could feel herself blushing. She wasn't sure why. Something about the way his eyes locked on hers?

"Guess you have a lot of time for daydreaming in this job," Patrick said.

She shrugged. "Once the breakfast crowd leaves, it gets kinda quiet."

His grin grew wider. "And what do you daydream about?"

She grinned back at him. "Things that are none of your business."

"Didn't you daydream this morning that a nice guy was going to come in, order ham and eggs, and ask you out for Friday night?"

"Is that what you want?" Destiny pulled out her pad. Why was her hand shaking like that? She suddenly felt fluttery. "Ham and eggs?"

She looked up to see his dark eyes trained on hers. "Yes, that's what I want. Ham and eggs. And for you to go out with me Friday night."

"And how do you want the eggs?" Destiny couldn't remove her eyes from his gaze. It was as if he held her there, froze her with those deep, dark-jeweled eyes.

Suddenly, she felt very frightened. *This isn't right. Something very wrong is happening here. I feel like . . . a prisoner.*

"Scrambled, please," he said. "And could I have a toasted bagel with that? And what time should I pick you up Friday night?"

His eyes . . . the stare was so intense, it made Destiny's head hurt.

Then slowly the pain faded. And she felt comfortable again. No. More than comfortable. She felt as if everything was floating. As if she were floating off the floor. And the whole diner became soft, and shimmering, and bright. *Not real . . . not real at all.*

And she saw things in Patrick's eyes. She saw clouds and

blue sky, and a pale, white moon, fluffy like tissue paper, round and full.

A full moon in Patrick's eyes. And he was saying something to her. But she was floating now, and he was so far away, his voice so distant and muffled.

What was he saying?

Something about Harrison.

No. Harrison and I don't have an exclusive arrangement. No, Patrick, I'm free to go out with anyone I want. Yes, I'd love to see you Friday. Can you pick me up at home?

Yes, that would be great.

And what will we do Friday night?

She struggled to hear his voice, muffled by a strong wind, the wind that blew behind the full moon in his eyes. All that blue sky, so clear and bright, and the full moon trembling in the middle of it.

What did you say? You want to take me into Drake Park, sink your fangs into my throat, and feed on my warm blood?

Oh, yes. Excellent. That sounds awesome.

Yes. I'm definitely up for that.

And then Destiny felt as if she were sinking. Suddenly heavy, she dropped from the clouds. The blue sky faded away, taking the full moon with it. And she stood heavily behind the counter, leaning on the yellow Formica, in the darkness of the diner, the smell of grease and bacon invading her nose, and stared at the young man with the dimples, sitting on the stool across from her.

What was his name? Patrick?

Yes. Patrick and I are going out Friday night after work. I'll have to be careful not to let Harrison know.

"I'll get those eggs," Destiny said, taking the menu from Patrick. "Anything to drink?"

"Just your blood."

He didn't say that. Destiny, why are you making up these things? Why can't you concentrate this morning?

"Coffee," he said. "Black is fine."

"You got it," she said.

"I'm looking forward to Friday," Patrick called after her.

chapter thirty-three

HARRISON
AND LIVVY

LIVVY MET HARRISON AT THE CINEPLEX AT THE DARK Springs Mall at eight o'clock. A warm night, the air heavy and wet. She wore a white shirt over a sleeveless green tank top and white shorts. Something Destiny would wear.

She had put on clear lip gloss, a dab of peach-colored eye shadow. Totally boring, Livvy thought. But Destiny likes that clean-cut, all-American-girl look.

Can I fool Harrison into thinking I'm my sister? Livvy watched him climb out of his car and come hurrying toward her. Well, Harrison was totally clueless at that party. No reason to think he'll figure it out tonight.

I'll bet Destiny hasn't even told him about me.

Afraid she'll frighten him away by making her family seem too weird.

Well, guess what, Harrison, my boy? You *should* be frightened. Because an evil vampire is out to get you—namely me.

Tonight I'm going to start getting you ready. No big deal, guy. A few sips of blood from your lovely throat. You'll hardly feel it, a big healthy hunk like you.

So sweet . . . I know you're going to taste so sweet.

Once we get started, we won't want to stop, will we? Sunday night is the full moon. That's your big night, Harrison. Sunday night when the moon is at its height, you and I will hook up in the best way.

We will mix our blood. I'll drink yours and you'll drink mine. It's so sexy and so delicious and so . . . *hot*, Harrison. Wait and see.

I'm getting all tingly just thinking about Sunday night.

Oh, wow. I just want a taste. I'm *dying* for a taste, Harrison. Can you see how much I want you?

He's so cute and nice and . . . sincere. That's why you like him, isn't it, Dee? That's why he's your new guy.

Well, how are you going to like him after Sunday night when he's one of us? A vampire, Dee. Your summer hunk is going to be a vampire.

Will you still go to his house parties? Still hang out with him on campus?

I don't think so.

Hey, don't blame me, sister. It's all *your* fault. I'm just paying you back. You murdered Ross. You came into my building at dawn and murdered my boyfriend.

Did you really think I would just hang back and not do anything at all?

You're going to pay, Dee. Patrick and I will see to that.

Where are you tonight? Probably home thinking you're safe and sound. Well, Patrick will be there soon. Sunday night the two of you will mix *your* blood under the light of the full moon.

Then you can rejoin Harrison—forever. You can have him forever, Dee, because you'll be an immortal too.

The perfect revenge? I think so.

And then Patrick and I . . .

Patrick and I . . .

Livvy pictured Patrick, tall and strong. A leader. Smart and quick.

But with those dimples. Those adorable dimples and the wavy, brown hair. Is he to die for? Yes.

She thought about the way he held her so tightly, as if she were his prisoner. And she thought about his kisses, tender for only a second, and then so hard, so hard and passionate, they hurt.

Blood on my lips. As if he *wanted* to hurt me.

Cruel kisses. Exciting and frightening at the same time.

Like Patrick.

And now Harrison came trotting up to her, jamming his car keys into his jeans. He flashed her a smile. "Hey, Dee. Am I late?"

"No. Right on time."

"You look great."

"Thanks."

He motioned to the movie theater. "So you want to see something tonight?"

Livvy wrapped her arm in his. She licked her lips. "Wouldn't you rather take a walk?"

chapter thirty-four

DESTINY
AND PATRICK

DESTINY BALANCED THE CORDLESS PHONE ON HER shoulder as she used her hands to check the oven. "Dad, I thought you were coming home tonight," she said into the phone.

"I can't, Dee." Dr. Weller sounded tired, his voice hoarse. "We're down to the crunch here."

"The crunch? What do you mean?"

"Sunday night is the full moon. My hunters and I are going into that abandoned apartment building at dawn Monday morning. I've got to get everyone prepared. I—"

"Hold on a sec, Dad," Destiny said. "Mikey's pizza is burning."

She pulled on oven mitts and lifted the pizza tray from the oven. Then she carried it over to the white Formica kitchen counter. "Hey, Mikey—it's almost dinnertime!" she shouted. "It just has to cool."

She lifted the phone back to her ear. "Dad? Are you still there? I'm terrified about this whole thing. Do you really have to go into that building?"

Destiny never told her father that she'd already been inside it. Never told him how strange and frightening it was with vampires—dozens of them—settled in the empty apartments.

She knew he'd be furious that she took such a risk.

But now *he* was determined to take an even bigger risk. To attack the vampires in the building at dawn as they slept, to kill as many as he could.

"Dad, do you really think these vampires will just keep on sleeping as you wipe them out one by one? Don't you think they might fight back?"

A long silence at the other end.

"We've taken all precautions," he replied finally. "We'll be heavily armed against them. We're going to surprise them, Dee. They won't know what hit them."

"But, Dad—"

"I can't talk about it, Dee. When is Mrs. Gilly supposed to come take care of Mikey?"

"At seven. I hope she comes on time. I'm going out tonight."

"With Harrison?"

"No. A new guy. I met him at the diner."

Why am I going out with a new guy? What about

Harrison? What if he finds out? Why did I say yes to Patrick?

Destiny couldn't remember.

"Well, make sure Mikey eats his dinner," Dr. Weller said. "And tell him—"

Destiny's phone beeped.

"Dad, I have another call. Can you hold on one sec?"

She pressed the flash button and waited for the second caller to come on. "Hello?"

"It's Mrs. Gilly, Dee. Hi."

"Oh, hi. I have my dad on the other line, so—"

"I'm terribly sorry. I can't come tonight to take care of Mikey. My cousin Jill is sick, and I have to hurry over there."

"Oh." Destiny's brain raced. That means I can't go out. I have to stay and take care of Mikey. "Sorry about your cousin. Thanks for calling."

Mrs. Gilly hung up after a few more apologies.

Mikey entered the room, stood on tiptoes to sniff the pizza on the counter, and went to the fridge. "Sit down," Destiny told him. "I'll slice your pizza for you."

She realized she'd forgotten about her dad. She clicked the phone. "Are you still there? Mrs. Gilly can't come. I'll stay with Mikey."

"What about your date?" Dr. Weller asked. "Can you call him?"

"Uh . . . no." Why didn't she get Patrick's cell number? "Guess I'll just have to tell him when he gets here. Well . . .

bye, Dad. I'd better—HEY!"

She let out a shout as she saw the red liquid puddling over the kitchen floor.

"Mikey—stop it! Are you crazy? Dad—he's pouring a big can of tomato juice on the floor. Mikey—stop! Put it down!"

"It isn't juice!" Mikey screamed. "It's BLOOD! It's BLOOD!"

Patrick arrived a little after seven-thirty. Destiny met him at the door. "Ready to rock?" he asked, flashing her his smile. He wore a black T-shirt under an open white sport shirt, straight-legged black denims.

Destiny shook her head. "I'm really sorry, Patrick. I didn't know how to get in touch with you. I have to stay and take care of my little brother."

Patrick's smile faded. "Oh. Wow. I'm sorry." His dark eyes flashed. "Hey, no problem. I'll stay and take care of the little guy with you."

Destiny could hear Mikey up in his room shouting about something. She had to fight him away to clean up the tomato juice. Then he refused to eat his pizza because he said the pepperonis were bugs.

"I don't think so," she told Patrick. "Mikey's being really difficult tonight. I think he needs *all* my attention."

Patrick sighed. Destiny felt the weight of his eyes on her. And once again she began to feel as if she were floating off the ground.

"How about Sunday night, Destiny?" Patrick asked. His voice seemed so muffled and far away. "Sunday is the night of the full moon. We could have fun Sunday night. Are you free?"

Destiny tried to focus, but everything was a blur. Finally, she turned away, lowered her gaze from his, and started to feel normal again.

"Yes. Sunday night," she repeated. "Okay, Patrick. Sorry about tonight. See you Sunday."

She started to close the door, but Patrick pulled it open again. He brought his face close to hers, and once again she fell under the spell of his eyes.

"I'm going to drink your blood Sunday night," Patrick whispered. "And you will drink mine. We'll have such a nice night, Destiny."

Then he wiped her mind clean and pulled his face from hers.

"Sounds great," Destiny said. "Can't wait, Patrick. See you Sunday."

chapter thirty-five

AN EVIL
CREATURE
OF THE NIGHT

"WHOA! I FEEL GREAT!"

Harrison came bursting into the diner. He started dancing in front of Destiny, shaking his booty, hands high above his head.

Destiny stood behind the counter, a stack of dirty plates in her hands.

"I feel great! I feel so great!" Harrison exclaimed.

A few customers laughed. Mr. G. stuck his head out through the window from the kitchen. "You're the fry cook, remember?" he called. "Not the entertainment. Get back here before you scare all my customers away."

Grinning, Harrison ducked under the counter. He took the stack of plates from Destiny and kissed her on the cheek.

"Harrison, are you losing it?" she whispered. "What's your problem?"

"I'm in a totally awesome mood," he said. "Is that a problem?"

He tried to kiss her again. Destiny saw Mr. G. watching them and slid away.

Harrison handed the dirty plates through the window to Mr. G. Destiny picked up her order pad and went to talk to two customers in the booth near the window.

When she returned, Harrison was still grinning at her. He brought his face close to hers. "That was great last night," he whispered.

She stared at him. "Excuse me?"

"Order?" Mr. G. poked his head out the window.

"Oh, yeah." Destiny lowered her eyes to her pad. "Two All-Americans with ham, hold the potatoes, white toast."

She pulled down two white coffee mugs, moved to the coffee-maker, and filled them with the steaming hot coffee. She put the mugs on a tray with a small milk pitcher and carried it to the two men in the booth.

Harrison grinned at her again. "Didn't you hear me? I just said I had a great time last night. That was really so totally excellent. I mean—"

Destiny narrowed her eyes at him. "Have you lost your mind? Last night?"

Oh, no. She had a sudden feeling of dread. It tightened her stomach and made her head spin for a moment.

Last night?

And then she saw the two tiny red points on Harrison's throat.

And she knew.

Livvy. Again.

Livvy was coming after Harrison. First Ari, now Harrison.

But why?

Didn't Ross tell Livvy how much I still care about her? That I'll do anything to help her and bring her back to us? Didn't Ross tell her?

Why is she going after Harrison?

Destiny spun away from him. She couldn't bear to see the two wounds on his neck.

There's only one reason why Livvy is doing this, she decided. She trembled so hard she had to grab the counter to hold herself up. Only one reason . . .

She is beyond saving. She has truly become one of them . . . an evil creature of the night.

chapter thirty-six

AN UNEXPECTED MURDER

"DOES MY HAIR LOOK OKAY?" LIVVY ASKED. "I NEVER realized I'd miss mirrors so much."

"It looks fine," Monica said, brushing the back of Livvy's hair with her hand. "That purple lipstick looks really hot."

Livvy snickered. "It used to drive my family crazy. One night my dad asked me why I wanted to look like a Halloween witch."

Suzie sighed. "You were lucky. My dad never paid that much attention to me. He'd never comment on my lipstick or . . . anything."

"I miss my mom and dad," Monica said, turning to the window. "They didn't deserve me. They deserved someone better."

Livvy gave her a gentle shove. "Hey, don't get down on

yourself. You have your good qualities, you know. You're a really good friend. You're kind. You're generous . . ."

"And I'm a vampire," Monica said. She shrugged. "I made my choice, right? But sometimes I wonder."

"You're just hungry," Suzie said, adjusting the top of her striped tube top. "We're all hungry."

"Party night!" Livvy exclaimed.

"*Every* night is party night, right?" Monica said, but without much enthusiasm.

"Hey, are you still feeding on that guy, Alby?" Livvy asked.

Suzie grinned. "Yeah. Both of us. Monica and I have been sharing him." She giggled. "He doesn't have a clue."

"Tomorrow night is the full moon," Livvy said, carefully applying purple eye shadow over her lids.

"Duh. Tell us about it," Monica said.

Livvy turned to them. "Are you going to make Alby a vampire?"

Suzie shrugged. "Why not? He's so cute."

Monica turned to Livvy. "What about that mystery guy you've been chasing after?"

"He's toast," Livvy replied. "Tomorrow night, he starts to live the good life."

Monica squinted at her. "Is he really hot? Why are you so into him?"

An evil smile spread slowly over Livvy's pale face. "Because he was my sister's boyfriend." She laughed.

Monica shook her head. "Weird. All three of us still have family problems."

Livvy shook her head. "No problem," she said softly. "No problem at all."

As a bat, Livvy swooped low over her old house. Through the front window, she glimpsed Destiny. Destiny on the couch and beside her . . . yes, Harrison.

Lucky guy.

Harrison with his arm around Destiny, the glow of the television washing over them, bathing them in dull reds and blues.

Ah, look. The two of them cuddling together.

What a sweet scene. Enjoy it, Harrison. Tomorrow night you will be mine. And Destiny will be Patrick's. And it will all change.

Your world will end. And a new one will begin.

Livvy raised her wings and swooped higher. One circle of the house, she thought. A house I'll never enter again.

The light was on in Mikey's room but the curtains covered the window. Livvy circled again and perched on the narrow window ledge outside her old room above the garage. The room Destiny and I shared . . . before the murdering . . . before the blood began to flow . . . before the *hunger*.

She saw her bed, carefully made. Her old stuffed leopard standing on the pillowcase as if on guard. The shelves of CDs against the wall beneath her Radiohead poster.

She felt a sudden pang—of what? Sadness? Loneliness? Longing for her old life?

No way.

No way. I don't feel anything. I'm just hungry, that's all.

But she pictured Ross. Sitting on the edge of her bed, the two of them wrapped up in each other. Her hands in his hair. His arms tight around her. Kissing her . . . kissing her for so long, until they were both breathless, until their lips were dry and chapped. Kissing and then . . .

No!

I don't want to remember any of this. I don't feel anything. Not anything.

She kicked off with her spindly bat legs, flapped her wings hard, feeling the warm air against her skin, and soared away from the house, high into the charcoal night sky.

She flew low over the trees, breathing the warm air, refreshing herself, sending all thoughts away, except for the thought of feeding. And on the edge of town, where the last tiny cottages stood, a few blocks from the rock quarry, she found a guy just waiting to feed her.

He stood beside his Harley motorcycle at the curb, shiny blue helmet in his hand, the light from the streetlamp revealing his shaved head, the bushy, dark mustache spread over his lips. Black vest over a black T-shirt, tight black jeans. Cowboy boots with big heels.

Livvy landed on the sidewalk in the next block and quickly transformed into her own body. She straightened her short skirt over her bare legs, adjusted her halter, and strolled up to the chopper dude.

"Hey, what's up?" she asked, gazing into his narrow, brown eyes.

He shrugged his broad shoulders.

The guy must work out twenty hours a day, Livvy thought. But he won't be strong enough to fight me off.

He grinned at her and patted the seat of the motorcycle. "Lookin' for a ride?"

"Not really."

She lowered her head and bulled into him and knocked him onto his back before he even realized what was happening. The blue helmet bounced down the sidewalk.

He let out a groan and started to lift himself to his feet. But Livvy was on top of him and sank her fangs into the tender skin under his chin. A howl of pain burst from his open mouth. But it faded to a whisper as Livvy began to drink.

A few seconds later, he was sprawled on his back, whimpering like a frightened dog. Livvy had his arms pressed against the pavement. Her hair spread over his face as she drank, making loud sucking, lip-smacking sounds, grunting softly with pleasure as the thick, warm liquid oozed down her throat.

She stopped before she had her fill. She never could drink enough to be satisfied. That was the curse of it all, she knew. Never to be satisfied. Always to need more.

She climbed to her feet and wiped blood off her chin with the back of her hand. The guy lay sprawled on his back, half on the curb, half in the street. His eyes were shut and he was still whimpering.

Humming to herself, Livvy strode down the sidewalk a few yards, picked up his helmet, carried it back, and placed it on the guy's stomach. She licked her lips. She loved the taste of dried blood, so sharp and sweet at the same time.

"Bye, cutie." She transformed to a bat once again and took off without looking back.

She returned to the apartment building early. Dawn was still a few hours away.

I need my beauty sleep, she decided. Tomorrow night is the full moon—and my night to shine. A big night for Harrison, and for my sister. I want to be ready for it.

She stepped into the building in human form and made her way up the dimly lit staircase. On the first floor, rats scampered through piles of garbage. A tall stack of old newspapers teetered in the late-night breezes.

As Livvy walked past open apartment doors, she heard low moans, groans, and whispers. Orange light flickered in the apartment that Suzie and Monica shared.

Were they back? Were they still awake?

Livvy heard a scuffling sound. A hard *thud* from deep in the apartment.

Curious, she stepped into the doorway and squinted into the flickering light.

Oh, no. She pressed both hands over her mouth to stifle her cry.

Monica lay on her back on the floor, fully dressed, one

shoe on, one off. Her hands outstretched, legs apart—a wooden stake standing straight up. A wooden stake through her chest. Monica's head tilted at a harsh angle, eyes still open.

No. Oh, no.

Monica murdered in her own apartment.

Hands still pressed to her mouth, Livvy heard noises in the bedroom.

A scraping sound. A groan. A sharp cry.

A shiver of terror rolled down Livvy's body.

The murderer—he was still in the apartment!

chapter thirty-seven

THE REAL
MURDERER

HER LEGS RUBBERY AND WEAK, LIVVY STAGGERED
forward a few feet. Holding her breath, she stepped over one
of Monica's outstretched legs. Fighting off her panic, she
moved silently to the bedroom doorway. And peered inside.

Her breath caught in her throat when she saw the struggle in the bedroom. She pressed her back against the wall
and watched in silent horror as Patrick and Suzie battled.

"You're weak!" he cried, his face red, eyes bulging with
anger. "You're too weak. I can't let the weak ones survive!"

He slammed her into the wall as if she were weightless.
Suzie bounced off, let out a painful groan, and fell onto her
back on the cot.

Before she could move, Patrick raised a pointed stake
high over her body—and with both hands, swung it down

hard. Suzie let out a shrill scream as the stake penetrated her chest, drove through her heart, and poked out of her back with a loud sucking sound.

No! Livvy thought, frozen in terror, unable to move, unable to take her eyes away. *She's my friend . . . my friend!*

Suzie writhed and kicked, her hands and feet thrashing the air like a pinned insect. Patrick held the stake, thrust it deeper through her chest, gripping it with both hands, sliding it through her body.

Another cry from Suzie, weaker this time. She grabbed at the stake, tried to shove it away. But her strength was fading. And her body was beginning to disintegrate.

Her skin peeled off quickly. Large chunks fell off her arms, her face. Her eyeballs dropped from their sockets and rolled across the room. The flesh of her cheeks and forehead melted away, revealing bone underneath.

Her skeletal arms still grabbed for the stake, thrashed and swiped at it—until the bone began to disintegrate.

Livvy gaped in horror as Suzie's skull crumbled into powder. Her arms—just gray bone now—fell motionless to the floor and crumbled to chunks, then powder. In a few seconds, her crumpled clothing lay spread on the floor, no body inside, a few ashes blowing in the breeze from the window.

She was older than I thought, Livvy realized. *So old she crumbled to ashes. She . . . she didn't deserve to die like this.*

"Too weak," Patrick muttered, heaving the stake angrily against the wall. "I can't allow the weak ones to stay. I can't!"

A soft cry escaped Livvy's lips.

Did he hear it?

She didn't wait to see. She spun away and started to run. Stumbling over Monica's body in the living room, she caught her balance, and kept running.

She darted frantically down the long hall, tripping over garbage and piles of newspaper. Breathing hard by the time she reached the stairs, she grabbed the metal rail and pulled herself up, forced her legs to carry her higher.

Gasping for breath, she reached the second floor, and ran blindly to her apartment halfway down the hall. Into the warm darkness, a hot breeze from the open window area.

Into the darkness and safety of the bedroom where she stood shivering, hugging herself tightly. She shut her eyes and gritted her teeth, forcing her body to stop its trembling.

But she couldn't shut out the picture of Patrick, shoving the stake through Suzie's chest, the fury that twisted his face, the sick sound the stake made as it poked through Suzie's body. Her bony hands in the air as if begging . . . begging for mercy.

Livvy's stomach lurched. She felt sick. She stumbled to the glassless window hole, leaned out, and vomited up some of the blood she had drunk—her dinner. It had tasted so sweet going down. Now it sickened her, sour and acid.

Still gagging, she heard a sound behind her. Wiping her mouth with the back of her hand, she turned to the door.

Patrick?

No. The footsteps passed. Some other vampire returning home after a night of feeding.

Livvy kicked off her shoes and climbed into bed. She pulled the blanket over her head and tried to stop shaking. But how could she stop thinking about her two dead friends?

Patrick. Patrick murdered them.

He's weeding out the weak.

And that means . . . *Patrick killed Ross*.

Buried under her blanket as if in a dark, warm cocoon, Livvy's mind whirred. It was coming clear to her. The horror of her situation. The danger she was in.

It all began to come clear.

Destiny didn't murder Ross. Patrick murdered Ross because he was weak. Because he wanted to see his parents, because he was homesick.

Patrick is the murderer. He is killing his own.

Destiny is innocent. She probably came here to warn me. Or just to plead with me to give up this life and come home so Dad can cure me.

And now I've agreed to let Patrick go after Destiny, to let him turn my sister into a vampire, too. And I agreed to trick her boyfriend into exchanging blood and becoming an immortal.

Livvy gasped. It's all a test. Patrick is testing me.

And do I have a choice? I have to go through with it.

If I try to stop Patrick from attacking Destiny, then he will know that I am weak.

And he will kill me too.

part seven

NIGHT OF
THE FULL MOON

chapter thirty-eight

HARRISON'S
BIG DATE

HARRISON GAZED UP AT THE FULL MOON AS HE PULLED his car to a stop. The moon floated low in the blue-black evening sky. It had rained earlier in the day. And now the moonlight was reflected in dozens of puddles and tiny pools all along the road, making the whole earth seem to sparkle.

Unreal.

Harrison slapped his hands on the steering wheel in rhythm to the dance music beat on the car stereo. He sang along, waiting for the light to change to green.

He thought about Destiny. Also unreal.

Picturing her made his heartbeats drum, almost as fast as the music. She had been different lately. So much needier. So much sexier.

Harrison flashed back to the other night. Destiny kissing him, kissing him so passionately, pressing herself against him, moving her hands through his hair.

And making those little sighs, the soft moans. Kissing his face . . . his neck. Yes. Kissing his neck.

It was all so unreal.

Harrison touched the little bite marks on his throat. Destiny had really gotten carried away.

Man, she was suddenly so *hot*!

The light changed. Harrison lowered his foot to the gas pedal. He couldn't wait to see her tonight. She had promised him something special.

Something special . . .

He knew what that meant. And now, his heartbeats were drumming *faster* than the music on the radio!

He turned onto Union Street. He could see the entrance to the mall up ahead. They planned to meet where they met last time in front of the Cineplex.

Harrison brought the car around to the front of the movie theater and ducked his head to search for Destiny through the passenger window.

No. Not here. Where was she?

He checked the dashboard clock. Eight-thirty-six.

Destiny said she'd be here at eight-thirty.

Yes. Eight-thirty. She said she had a nice surprise for him. But she wanted to give it to him when the full moon was high in the sky.

Unreal.

What did the full moon have to do with anything? Why was Destiny being so mysterious?

He glanced up at the moon. Higher in the sky now,

more golden than orange, with a single wisp of black cloud cutting it off in the middle.

"Dee, where are you?"

He drove past the theater, turned and pulled into a parking place between two SUVs. He drummed his fingers on the wheel. Checked his wallet to make sure he'd remembered to bring some money. Gazed up at the full moon again, hazy behind a thin film of cloud. Then back at the clock—eight-forty-five.

Destiny was always on time. This was not like her.

Leaving the car running, Harrison climbed out and stood in front of it, searching under the bright lights at the front of the Cineplex. He saw a short line of people in front of the box office. Two teenage girls waiting for someone at the side of the theater.

No one else. No Destiny.

I want my special surprise, Destiny. I want you to keep your promise. Where are you? You don't want to keep me here in suspense, do you?

He took a few steps away from the car. "Hey—!" He saw a couple of guys he knew going into the theater. He waved to them and called out, but they didn't see him. They vanished inside.

Harrison strode back to the car and dropped behind the wheel. Almost nine o'clock. Maybe she got hung up. Maybe she couldn't make it for some reason. No. She'd call. Maybe she was in an accident or something.

Harrison sighed. He hated to wait for people. It always made him very tense. Most of his friends showed up half an hour late to everything, and it drove him crazy. He was always on time. That probably drove his friends crazy!

He picked up his cell phone. He stared at it for a few moments. Nine-oh-seven on the clock. He punched in Destiny's cell number. And listened to four rings. Then her voicemail message: "This is Destiny. Leave a message, okay?" The long beep.

He clicked off the phone.

Where is she?

He tried her cell number again. Maybe the phone was buried in her bag, and she didn't hear it. Again, he listened to four rings. When her message came on, he clicked off the phone and tossed it onto the seat.

He climbed out of the car, slamming the door behind him. He paced back and forth in front of the movie theater for a while.

At nine-thirty, he climbed back into the car. He gazed up at the full moon, high in the sky now, a bright, silvery circle. Then he backed out of the parking place.

Where are you, Destiny? Did you stand me up?

That's so not like you.

Harrison felt his muscles tighten, felt a weight in the pit of his stomach. This wasn't like Destiny at all.

Something must be wrong. Something must be terribly wrong.

He sped out of the mall and turned left on Union Street.

He decided to drive to Destiny's house. He had to find out what was going on.

chapter thirty-nine

DESTINY
SURPRISES PATRICK

PATRICK COULDN'T TAKE HIS EYES OFF DESTINY'S throat.

The skin pale and smooth, like velvet. Her neck long and straight. He could taste it. He could taste that spot just under her chin, that soft spot without muscle where the veins ran free and close to the skin.

As they danced, he watched the veins throb, a subtle blue against the smooth, soft skin. She said something to him, shouting over the loud music. But he didn't hear her. He was concentrating so hard on the tiny, throbbing veins, on her delicious throat.

Soon, Destiny, you and I will be together forever, he thought, returning her smile.

The beat changed as the DJ worked his mix. Destiny changed her rhythm and Patrick changed with her, moving his body slowly now, bumping against her. Any excuse to touch her. Eyes on her throat. If only he could sink his teeth into that soft skin right this minute and drink . . . drink until she moaned and sighed.

He knew the full moon was high in the sky by now. The dance club had no windows. But Patrick could *feel* the moon above him. His excitement rose with the moon. And so did his hunger.

Destiny's face held its smile as she danced under the flashing lights over the dance floor. She's gentler than her sister, Patrick decided. She has a sweetness about her—an innocence?—that Livvy doesn't have.

He wondered how Livvy was doing with Destiny's boyfriend, Harrison. She seemed so eager to go after him, so eager to take him under the moonlight and turn him into a vampire.

Did she hate her sister *that* much?

Patrick wondered why. He wondered why one twin chose the vampire life—and the other had to be forced into it.

Tonight . . .

I will force her tonight. She won't know what is happening until it is too late.

What drove the sisters apart? Why does Livvy carry such anger against her twin?

And then as he danced, his thoughts changed, and he thought about the group of vampires he had joined. So many weaklings and fools who were endangering the whole group. Patrick knew the Hunters were organizing. He knew the Hunters would soon find their hiding place and try to drive them out.

He had to weed out the weaklings before the battle began.

He intended to win this battle. For nearly a hundred years, he had been driven from town to town. Forced to flee, to hide.

No more.

He intended to take a stand here. If the Hunters think they can chase us away so easily, bring them on. We'll be ready.

But first, he had to make sure everyone was strong.

Will you come through for me tonight, Livvy? Will you complete the job on Harrison? Or will you let him go, and prove that you are also one of the weaklings?

Patrick knew he didn't want to kill Livvy. He was attracted to her, drawn to her—to her sister too. But if he had to, he would kill Livvy the same way he had killed her friends.

We're going to be strong, strong enough to kill any Hunters that invade our homes.

He turned to Destiny. He realized she was squeezing his arm. "Patrick, what's wrong? You have such an unhappy look on your face."

"I . . . was thinking about something," he said. He took her hand and led her off the dance floor. "Enough dancing? I've worked up a real sweat." He picked up a cocktail napkin from the bar and mopped his forehead.

"That DJ is great," Destiny said. "That's why I like this club."

"Let's get some fresh air," Patrick said. He guided her through the crowd and out the front door. He heard shouts and saw a group of people in the parking lot. "What's going on?"

They followed the path to the parking lot. "An accident," Destiny said. "Someone backed an SUV into that Mini."

"Ooh." Patrick made a face. "The Mini is wrecked. Why didn't the SUV pick on someone his own size?"

A tall man in a wrinkled suit was screaming at the parking valet and shaking his fist in the air. Two women were screaming at him.

"Let's get out of here," Patrick said. He glanced up at the full moon. "It's such a nice night. Would you like to take a walk?"

Destiny smiled and took his arm. "Nice. Do you know Drake Park?"

He shook his head. "Not really."

"There's a path I like to walk. It's real pretty at night, especially under a full moon." Destiny glanced up at the moon too. "It leads to a pretty little creek."

"Let's go," Patrick said. He suddenly felt so hungry, he wiped a gob of drool off his chin and hoped Destiny didn't see.

They drove to Drake Park. Patrick kept a hand gently on her shoulder as they made their way along the twisting, dirt path, through thickets of tangled trees and low shrubs, to the creek.

As they walked, Destiny talked about her job at the diner, about her father, a veterinarian, and about her little brother, Mikey. Patrick didn't listen. His hunger had become a roar in his ears, like a pounding ocean wave crashing again and again.

He couldn't hear her. He could think only of his thirst, of the gnawing in his stomach, the ache . . . the ache . . .

The moon had risen high in the sky. It filled the creek with silver light which made the narrow, trickling stream shimmer and glow.

Destiny took his hand. She gazed at the sparkling water. "Isn't it beautiful?"

"Yes," he managed. He knew he couldn't hold back much longer. "Yes, it is."

She squeezed his hand. "With the moon lighting the water, it's almost as bright as day."

"Yes," he agreed again. His fangs slid down over his lips.

Destiny was staring at the creek. "I've done all the talking," she said. "You haven't told me a thing about yourself."

"Well . . ." His brain was spinning now. All dazzling bright lights and wild, throbbing music. The hunger so strong he wanted to toss back his head and howl.

Instead, he grabbed Destiny by the shoulders. Lowered his face to her throat. Dug his fangs deep into the soft flesh of her throat.

He dug deeper, making loud sucking sounds, holding her tightly, pressing his forehead into her chin.

And then with a cry of disgust, he staggered back. Dizzy, his stomach heaving. "Noooooo." A sick moan escaped his throat. He lurched away from her, bent over, and started to retch.

chapter forty

LIVVY
SURPRISES PATRICK

"YOU'RE . . . NOT . . . DESTINY," HE WHISPERED when he could finally talk. He stood up straight and shook himself.

She hadn't moved the whole while. Moonlight washed over her, making her blond hair gleam, making it appear that she was standing in a spotlight.

"You're Livvy, aren't you," he accused.

"Patrick, you're such an ace," she replied. "Really sharp. You just pick up on things so fast, don't you?"

He stared at her in disgust, holding his hands in front of him as if shielding himself from her. "What are you doing here, Livvy?"

"My sister decided she didn't want to go out with you. She said you're just not her type. But I didn't want you to be lonely."

Patrick narrowed his eyes at her. "Are you crazy?" He pointed to the moon. "You know you have an assignment tonight."

Livvy shrugged.

His anger grew quickly. "Don't you realize how dangerous it is to play this trick on me? To disobey me? What about Harrison, Livvy? What about your assignment?"

"Oh, I stood him up. I gave myself a new assignment," she said. Her body tensed. Her smile faded.

Patrick scowled. "What the hell are you talking about?"

"I brought something from home," Livvy said. "I brought it out here to the woods earlier . . . just for you. A surprise."

She bent behind a tree, grabbed something in both hands, and swung to face him.

"It's the stake," Livvy said, her voice trembling now, her face tight with fury. "The stake you used to kill my friends."

Patrick's hands flew up. His eyes bulged in shock.

She raised the stake high—and, with a loud cry, thrust it into his chest.

But he moved quickly, stumbling back. He grabbed the stake before it could penetrate his skin. Grabbed it in both hands and struggled to wrench it away from Livvy.

He caught her off-balance, still moving forward in her attempt to stab him. Now she gripped one end of the stake, and he gripped the other.

Patrick swung the stake hard and sent her spinning against a tree.

Livvy let out a cry as the stake flew out of her hands.

She shoved herself off the tree trunk and spun to face Patrick.

"Nice try," he said breathlessly. "But not nice enough."

He raised the stake in both hands—and cracked it in half over his thigh. Then he kept the pointed end and tossed away the other half.

"I've given *myself* a new assignment," he said, moving in on Livvy. He raised the pointed stake in one fist. "Can you guess what it is?"

chapter forty-one

A VAMPIRE
MUST DIE

HE BROUGHT THE STAKE DOWN HARD AND FAST, aimed at Livvy's heart.

She transformed into a bat, and the point sailed past her, barely grazing a wing. With a loud screech, she brought her wings up and sailed over Patrick's head. Then she stuck out her talons—and swooped down.

Hissing and shrieking, she scratched at his eyes.

He let out a cry of pain and stumbled back.

She scraped his cheeks with her talons. Blood streamed down his face.

With a groan, he swiped her hard with the back of his hand. His hand caught her in the belly, knocking her air out.

Stunned, Livvy toppled to the ground.

She gazed up in time to see Patrick raise a shoe to trample her. She scuttled out just as the heel slammed the ground.

Flapping her wings hard, she shot back into the air. He had dropped the stake and was bent, searching for it.

Livvy swooped to the ground behind him, transformed back into her own body, and grabbed up the stake as Patrick spun around.

"No—" he uttered as she slammed the stake with all her strength into his throat.

A sick cry burst from his open mouth as the stake poked through the skin, deep into his neck. His eyes bulged, and he grabbed for the stake with both hands.

But Livvy was too fast for him this time. She tugged the stake out, staring at the gaping hole in his neck. Then she slammed it into his body again, thrusting the point into his chest, into his heart.

He fell back, cracking his head on a tree trunk.

He didn't utter a sound. He stared up at Livvy as he collapsed onto his back. His legs folded, and his arms dropped limply to his sides, and didn't move.

A shaft of silver moonlight washed over the stake, tilted up in the air now as Patrick lay on his back, not moving. And then his skin started to melt and crumble away. Big chunks dissolving quickly, revealing the bones underneath.

Struggling to catch her breath, her chest heaving up and down, Livvy turned her back on him.

I don't want to see what happens to him.

I killed him.

I killed him because he killed my friends. And I killed him to save my sister.

Livvy felt upset now, confused. She didn't feel as if she'd scored any kind of victory.

What will happen next?

Her thoughts turned to Destiny.

Have I saved you tonight, Dee?

Or have I killed you too?

chapter forty-two

"ONE LAST KISS . . . BEFORE I KILL YOU"

DR. WELLER STOOD TREMBLING IN THE ABANDONED apartment building, listening to the screams of agony all around him.

Vampires were dying. His hunters were working fast, catching them while they slept in their open apartments, piercing their hearts with wooden stakes, and quickly moving to the next apartment.

Dr. Weller had trouble moving as quickly. He had killed one vampire in his bed, a young man with dried blood caked down his chin. He had thrust his pointed stake between the young man's ribs, watched him come awake, eyes bulging in disbelief. Listened to his scream of pain as he realized what had happened to him. Then watched him die.

He's not really a human, Dr. Weller told himself. He's a creature now, an evil creature in a human body. He preyed on living humans, innocent humans. He ruined lives. He deserves to die.

But now as the sun began to rise in the glassless windows of the unfinished building, Dr. Weller stood trembling in front of a low cot, unable to act, unable to move or think straight.

This is not a human, he told himself, staring at the sleeping girl in the long, black nightshirt. This is an evil creature now.

He gripped the stake tightly in his right hand. His left hand was raised to his feverish forehead.

This is an evil, inhuman creature now.

But she is my daughter.

He gazed down at Livvy, gazed through the tears that blurred his eyes, that ran down his cheeks. This is my daughter, and I have no choice—I have to kill her.

I am the leader of the Hunters, and I have vowed to rid Dark Springs of these blood-sucking killers.

A vampire murdered my wife, their mother.

And now I'm about to lose another precious family member to the evil ones.

Dr. Weller raised his eyes and cursed the sky.

His stomach tightened. For the second time that night he felt he might retch.

How can I kill my own daughter?

Could I ever face Destiny again? Mikey?

Could I ever tell them the truth: *I killed your sister. I killed Livvy with my own hands.*

I . . . I can't, Dr. Weller thought. He staggered back from the cot, his eyes on his sleeping daughter. Her blond hair flowed over the pillow. Her fair skin caught the glow of the red morning sun from the window.

I can't do this. It's asking too much of any man.

I'm not a coward. I'm a brave man. Here I am in this apartment building, risking my life, attacking vampires where they live. No, I'm not a coward.

But . . .

He heard a high, shrill scream from down the hall. A girl's scream. Another vampire murdered by one of his hunters.

A high wail of pain floated down the hall. Another victim of the hunters.

Dr. Weller gripped the walkie-talkie attached to his belt. So far, no calls for help. The operation seemed to be going flawlessly.

He sighed, staring down at his daughter's sleeping face.

I'm the one who should call for help.

I should call for one of my hunters. I should leave the room, whisper good-bye to Livvy, and leave the room. And let my hunter do the job we came here to do.

Can I do that?

Livvy stirred. She let out a soft sigh.

She turned toward him, eyes still closed.

It isn't really Livvy anymore, he decided. His heart

began to thud in his chest. *It isn't my daughter.*

He took a deep breath. Raised the stake high.

Changed his mind.

I just want to kiss her good-bye.

Kiss her good-bye . . . before I kill her.

And as he leaned his tear-stained face down to kiss her cheek, Livvy's hands shot up—and grasped him tightly around the neck.

"LIVVY—NO!" he shouted. "LET GO!"

She opened her eyes. "Don't do anything, Dad!" she cried, holding onto his neck, wrapping her arms around his neck. "Don't, Dad! It isn't Livvy. It's me."

He blinked. Stared hard at her. "Destiny—?"

She nodded. She kissed his cheek, then let go of his neck. "I'm sorry, Dad. I didn't want to scare you. But I had no choice. I—"

"Destiny?" he repeated. "Destiny?"

She nodded. "Yes, it's me. I traded places with Livvy. I had to save her life."

chapter forty-three

THICKER
THAN BLOOD

LATER, DESTINY EXPLAINED TO HER FATHER. "LIVVY
and I planned it all last night. She risked her life by taking
my place with a vampire named Patrick."

"But why did you take her place in the apartment?" Dr.
Weller asked.

"I had to," Destiny replied. "Livvy risked her life for me.
I had to risk my life for her. It was the only way to prove to
her how much I want to save her."

"You took a terrible risk," Dr. Weller said. He poured
milk into his coffee mug, then slid the milk carton across
the table to Destiny.

"We couldn't really say it out loud. But we showed how
much we cared by risking our lives for each other," Destiny
said. "Crazy, huh?" She poured milk into her mug and took
a sip of coffee.

Dr. Weller stared at her across the kitchen table, thinking hard. He raised his hands from around his coffee mug. "Look at me. I'm still shaking. We've been home for half an hour, and I can't stop shaking."

Destiny lowered her head. "I'm sorry, Dad."

He grabbed her hand. "No. Don't say that. You did a very brave thing tonight."

"So did Livvy," Destiny replied.

Dr. Weller nodded. Behind his glasses, his eyes teared over. "Twins," he murmured. "Twins stick together, right?"

Destiny took a long sip of coffee. "Yes. Being sisters meant a lot more to both of us than . . . than anything else."

"And you hatched this plan last night?" he asked.

"Last night," Destiny said. "Livvy flew into my window. She explained that she was furious at me. She told me about Ross. She—"

Destiny stopped. Her voice broke. She raised her eyes to her father. "Ross is dead, Dad. Killed by another vampire."

"Oh, no," Dr. Weller whispered. "No . . ."

Destiny nodded. "Yes, he's dead. I suppose we have to tell his family. Livvy thought I murdered him. That's why she was so angry."

Dr. Weller shook his head. "Ross dead," he murmured. "He was a good guy. And Livvy could be dead too. If only—"

"She may be okay, Dad. I'm sure I'll hear from her again."

"Tell her to come home," Dr. Weller said. "Tell her if she

comes home, I'll work even harder on finding a cure. I'll do everything I can."

"I'll try, Dad. I'll try." She squeezed his hand. "But don't get your hopes up."

Destiny left out one part of the story. She didn't tell her father that she and Livvy planned to meet the next night in their room above the garage.

"Don't tell him," Livvy had insisted. "I'll come see you, but I just can't see Dad. Not yet."

Destiny had agreed. And now it was the next night. The night after the full moon and all the horror it brought.

Destiny paced back and forth in her room, clasping and unclasping her hands, feeling so tense she could barely think straight.

Did Livvy survive last night? Did she kill Patrick? Is she okay? Will she come? Will she keep her promise?

Dr. Weller was working late at his lab. Mikey was closed up in his room watching Nickelodeon.

A warm breeze ruffled the curtains in the open window. Destiny heard a car horn honking far down the block. White moonlight washed into the room and slanted across the carpet.

Hugging herself, Destiny stepped into the square of moonlight. Cold moonlight, she thought. Moonlight is always so silvery hard and cold.

The curtains fluttered again. A blackbird landed gently on the sill. It shook itself, raising its wings, then hopped onto the bedroom floor.

Destiny jumped back. The bird tilted its head, gazing up at her with its shiny black bead of an eye.

"Livvy—?" Destiny whispered.

The blackbird transformed quickly, its body rising, arms poking out where the wings had been . . . a head . . . blond hair. All so quick and silent.

In seconds, Livvy stood across from Destiny. She brushed back her hair and glanced around the long, narrow room they had shared. "You . . . haven't changed a thing," Livvy said. She picked up her stuffed leopard and pressed it against her cheek. "Everything is the same."

Destiny stared at her sister. Livvy wore a tight white midriff blouse over a black miniskirt. Long, red plastic earrings dangled from her ears. She had a tiny rhinestone stud in the side of her nose.

A laugh escaped Destiny's throat. "You haven't changed, either," she said. "I mean, you look exactly the same."

Livvy frowned. "I've changed a lot, Dee. Don't think I'm the same old Livvy." She tossed the leopard onto the bed.

"You . . . you're okay?" Destiny asked. "I mean, last night—"

"I killed him. I killed Patrick," Livvy said. "See? I'm not the same. I've *killed*, Dee. Do you believe it? I've killed."

Destiny let out a sob. "I'm just so glad you're okay." She rushed to her sister. They hugged, hugged each other tightly, pressing their cheeks against each other. Destiny's cheek was damp from her tears. Livvy didn't cry.

A voice from downstairs made them jump apart.

"Hey, who you talking to?" Mikey called up.

Livvy's eyes grew wide. She took a step toward the window. Destiny could see she was thinking of escape.

"No," she whispered to Livvy. "Let Mikey see you. He needs to see you and talk to you. You can help him, Liv."

Livvy looked doubtful, but she stayed.

"Come here, Mikey." Destiny went down and guided Mikey up the steps. "Livvy is here. She came back because she wants to see you."

As she and Mikey walked up the stairs, a feeling of panic swept over Destiny. *Maybe this isn't such a good idea. Maybe Mikey will totally freak.*

He stepped into the room. His eyes went from Destiny to Livvy. He froze.

"Mikey—" Destiny started.

Mikey took a few steps toward the two girls. He stared suspiciously at Livvy. He stopped a few feet away and studied her.

"Are you real?" he asked finally.

Livvy laughed. "Huh? Am I *what?*"

Mikey narrowed his eyes at her. "Are you real?" he repeated.

Livvy's expression softened. "Yes, Mikey, it's really me."

She hurried to him and wrapped him in a hug. Mikey burst into tears and began to sob at the top of his lungs.

"It's okay. It's okay," Livvy whispered, holding him. "It's okay, Mikey. Really. I love you. I still love you."

Destiny bit her bottom lip to keep from crying too. Would this help the poor little guy? Would it help him to know that Livvy was still around, still his sister, still loved him? Or would it make him even more sad and crazy?

Livvy held him until he stopped crying. Then he backed away from her, rubbing his eyes.

He studied her again. "Can you really fly?"

"No," she lied. "I'm just me. Really."

"But don't you fly and bite people in the neck?"

"No. I don't do that. That's *sick*," Livvy told him. "I . . . I just had to move out for a while. That's all."

He thought about what she said. Destiny couldn't tell if he believed Livvy or not.

"Are you coming back? Will you take me swimming?" he asked.

"Someday soon maybe. Not today," Livvy said.

They talked a while longer, with Livvy reassuring Mikey that she was normal and that someday she'd return. Livvy hugged Mikey again. Then Destiny took him to his room and put him to bed.

When she returned, Livvy stood staring out the window. "I have to go," she said. She shuddered. "Seeing Mikey . . . that was really hard."

"He seemed very happy," Destiny said. "I think maybe you helped him." She grabbed her sister's hand. "Don't go, Liv. I won't let you go again."

"Don't be stupid, Dee. I can't come back here. I've gone too far into the dark world. I can't return—even if I wanted to."

"Yes, you can," Destiny insisted. "Dad will find a cure. You *can* come back."

Livvy pushed Destiny's hand away. "Bye, Dee."

Her body began to shrink, so fast Destiny could hardly see the transformation. The wings sprouted . . . the black feathers . . . the spindly legs hopping on the carpet.

Livvy, a blackbird once again, jumped into the pool of silvery moonlight on the windowsill.

"Don't go! Please don't go!" Destiny shouted. She made a grab for the bird.

But Livvy took off, raised her wings high, and soared into the moonlight. Then she swerved sharply, and vanished into the darkness of the night.

"Don't go. Don't go. Don't go," Destiny whispered.

So close. I was so close to reaching Livvy, to convincing her to stay. So close . . .

She spun away from the window when she heard the doorbell downstairs.

She's back. She changed her mind. I *did* reach her!

Destiny raced down the stairs, taking them two at a time. She bolted through the kitchen, into the front hall.

The doorbell rang again.

"I'm coming. I'm coming, Liv."

Breathlessly, she pulled open the front door.

And stared at Harrison.

"Dee? Are you okay?"

She nodded. Struggled to catch her breath. "I ran the whole way from upstairs," she explained.

He squinted at her. "Where were you last night? You were supposed to meet me, remember? How come you didn't show?"

"Last night?" Destiny sighed. She pulled him into the house. "Harrison, that's a very long story . . ."